UNDER THE CAT'S EYE

A TALE OF MORPH AND MYSTERY

GILLIAN RUBINSTEIN

SIMON & SCHUSTER BOOKS FOR YOUNG READERS

ALSO BY GILLIAN RUBINSTEIN

Foxspell
Galax-Arena
Skymaze
Beyond the Labyrinth
Space Demons

SIMON & SCHUSTER BOOKS FOR YOUNG READERS
An imprint of Simon & Schuster Children's Publishing Division
1230 Avenue of the Americas, New York, New York 10020

Text copyright © 1998 by Gillian Rubinstein
Originally published in Australia in 1997 by
Hodder Headline Australia Pty Limited under the title *Under the Cat's Eye*.
First U. S. Edition, 1998

Book design by Anahid Hamparian
The text for this book is set in 12-Point Gilgamesh.
Printed and bound in the United States of America
10   9   8   7   6   5   4   3   2   1
Library of Congress Cataloging-in-Publication Data
Rubinstein, Gillian.
Under the cat's eye : a tale of morph and mystery / Gillian Rubinstein.
p. cm.
Summary: Jai and his friends at a boarding school join forces with shape-shifters
in their attempt to defeat the headmaster who steals the souls and futures of the students.
ISBN 0-689-81800-9
[1. Supernatural—Fiction. 2. Human-animal relationships—Fiction.
3. Boarding schools—Fiction. 4. Schools—Fiction. 5. Fantasy.] I. Title.
PZ7.R83133Un 1998
[Fic]—dc21   97-32643

FIRST
EDITION

This book is an homage to the authors of the books I read
and loved so much as a child, in particular John Masefield,
C. S. Lewis, Rudyard Kipling, Violet Needham,
and Robert Louis Stevenson, to whom I am indebted
for the name of "the oddity."

The ninth world of Nexhoath is based on the world of
children's books that I knew when I was growing up.
Echoes of my favorite authors will be found here.

This book is dedicated to their memory and to
Diana Wynne Jones.

One

They saw the sign before they saw the house.

NEXHOATH, it said in black Gothic letters. Underneath, in small neat print, was written: FAMILY-STYLE BOARDING SCHOOL FOR BOYS AND GIRLS. HEADMASTER: MR. M. M. DRAKE, BA MA.

Jai felt his stomach give a lurch, like the moment when you bicycle over the crest of a steep hill and there's nothing in front of you at all and your insides get left behind as you race downward. He peered anxiously out of the window, doing what he always did when he was nervous, adding together impossibly large numbers in his head: 32,426 plus 74,507 equals . . .

The car turned into the driveway, through the open iron gates, and chugged, the steam engine hissing slightly, over a little bridge. Jai's father was driving, hunched over the wheel, even more anxious and ill at ease than usual.

106,933, Jai said to himself.

The house came into view.

It sat squarely and heavily in the middle of a small park, its windows watchful like a hundred eyes. From its many chimneys smoke spiraled upward. Mist was rising from the damp ground under the trees. The smoke and the mist hung together in the still air as if they were waiting for something. Someone.

Jai was practical by nature. He liked facts and figures and he didn't really believe in intuition, but he was struck by a strong feeling that the house was watching and waiting for him. Something or someone there was expecting him. Even now they were looking out of the window to see if he had arrived yet. . . . 456,739 plus 901,238 equals . . .

He shook himself. 1,357,977. Of course they were expecting him. Letters had flown to and fro in an air of crisis. Somewhere had to be found for him to live, in a hurry. His parents had only a few more days before they had to leave the country. . . . He clenched his fists and bit into his lip.

"Splendid place," his father said in the falsely hearty voice he had been using ever since the first letter arrived. "Wonderful grounds!" He was so busy looking at the grounds that he stopped looking at the road.

"Oh, take care!" cried Jai's mother, and the car came to an abrupt halt, the steam brakes complaining with a loud whistle.

Two children had run out of the mist onto the driveway. One of them, a girl in a red cloak, had slipped and fallen in front of the car. The other, a boy also wearing red, ran back to help her up.

"Are you all right?" Jai's mother opened the door and began to get out.

"I didn't see them!" Jai's father was saying helplessly. "I just didn't see them."

"It's all right," said the boy. "We're all right. Honestly. Sorry." Then he spoke to the girl. "Come on, Seal!"

The girl got to her feet. She was laughing, trying not to. Jai stared at her. His last school, Sherbrooke, had been for boys only, and he didn't really know any girls. This girl had bright hazel eyes, and reddish-brown hair that stood out around her head like a flower's petals. He thought she looked nice. The boy looked all right, too, with dead-straight fair hair that fell over his forehead like water.

Neither of them took any notice of him. They said "sorry" several more times to his parents, brushed the mud off the girl's blue stockings, and ran off. He could hear them laughing as they disappeared into the mist.

"Wait," his mother cried, bending to pick something up from the gravel. "You dropped something! Children!"

But the children didn't hear her. She came back to the car and held the object out to Jai. "You take it, Jai. You can give it back when you see them."

The car started up again, and they moved forward. The near-accident had shaken Jai's father and he drove even more slowly than before. Jai had a few moments to study the thing his mother had handed him.

It was an oval ring or bangle, smooth, white, and hard like bone. On one side half an animal's face had been carved, and where the other half should have been was a blank impression, the size of a thumbprint. Jai put his thumb into it, against the fierce wild animal face. The feel of the bone made him shiver. He slipped it into his pocket.

The car stopped in front of the house. Jai's father let go of the wheel, his hands still white with tension. His mother took a deep breath as if she was going to speak. But she didn't say anything, just opened the car door.

Jai didn't move. He was thinking he could just stay in the car and it would turn around and make the journey back to the familiar house in the city. His father would park in the street, and they would go in, and his mother would exclaim about how cold it was, and set a match to the fire, and he would have a hot drink and settle down and do a math puzzle or maybe read one of his favorite books. His mother would light the lamps, and outside the gaslights in the street would come on. They would make the darkness safe and friendly, not like the darkness that was already falling around the strange, mysterious house.

But of course that was all impossible. Because everything had changed. His parents had to go away, for reasons he didn't quite understand, something to do with the Bureaucracy, and visas, and where you were born, and where you were allowed to live. He was all right, he had been born here, but his parents had been born in the other country, India, the one whose language they still spoke together at night, and now they had to go back to it. But Jai wasn't to go. They would come back for him when they had sorted everything out, and in the meantime he was going to stay here, at Nexhoath, the family-style boarding school for boys and girls.

"Come, Jai," his mother said in her gentle voice. She held out her hand to him, her bracelets sliding down her arm with a soft, utterly familiar tinkle. His father was blowing his nose with a huge white handkerchief, his face turned away. Jai immediately felt tears begin, but he fought them down. He was not going to cry. Sherbrooke boys never cried. He was going to be brave, like a proper Sherbrooke boy. He tipped his chin upward and set his face cheerfully as he stepped out of the car. He even managed a sort of smile as he studied the house in front of him.

It was built of gray stone. It had three rows of large windows topped by a roof of gray-blue slate and an elegant parapet. Set in the roof itself was another row of windows, smaller and less grand. From the gravel circle where the car had stopped, wide steps led to the front door. An animal-head knocker was set in the middle of the door, and on one side hung a bell rope.

"Look," Jai's mother said brightly. "So old-fashioned and quaint. Make the lion roar, Jai, and see who comes."

"Maybe a lion will arrive," his father said, trying to smile. Jai thought they must be feeling terrible to start making weak jokes and treating him as if he were a baby. He didn't think the animal was a lion anyway. He wasn't sure if it was even a real animal, but it looked fierce and untamable. As he stepped toward it he saw with a chill that the carving was the same as on the bone ring in his pocket. Only half the animal's face was carved. The other half was blank. He laid his palm for a moment on the blank part. It was smooth and cold. Then he lifted the head and knocked hard.

Bang, bang, bang, the noise echoed through the house. From far away he thought he could hear the faint sound of a dog barking.

"I'll get your suitcase." His father gulped and went to hide his face in the trunk of the car.

Below the animal head was a large embossed doorknob, and below that was the slit for letters. Jai bent down and looked through it. Inside it was quite dark, much darker than outside in the twilight. He squinted, turning his head slightly to see more. Something flashed in the darkness. Two green globes, like the eyes of an animal, seemed to be staring from a great distance straight into his eyes. He jumped away from the door. He imagined some fierce creature coming to open it. He backed down the steps. Then a line of light shone under the door, and they all heard footsteps.

With a loud creak the door opened.

"Mr. and Mrs. Kala. Good afternoon. Welcome. I am Mr. Drake." An immensely tall man with faded blond hair swept straight back from his forehead stepped out of the light, hand outstretched. "And this must be young Jai!"

He was one of those people who seem both young and old at the same time. His face was smooth and unlined, but his pale blue eyes looked ancient. His clothes were like a uniform, a black frock coat with epaulets and brass buttons, and black trousers with satin stripes down the sides. They appeared heavy and rigid, as if they were holding the man together and without them he would collapse in a heap.

"Jai, darling," his mother whispered, "remember your manners. Shake hands with Mr. Drake."

Mr. Drake's hand was bony, rough, and cold. He gripped Jai's hand as if he would never let go. "Welcome, my boy. Welcome to Nexhoath, your new home. We're delighted to have you here with us."

There was a moment's awkward silence.

"Well, say good-bye, son," Mr. Drake said. He added to Jai's parents, "Best not to draw these things out, you know. A clean, sharp separation is better for everyone."

Jai's father gulped again, gave Jai a brief, intense, wordless hug, and bolted for the car. His mother whispered to him in Hindi, the language of the other country, the one they would be going to without him. "Be brave, be good, never forget we love you and we are coming back as soon as we can."

"Ahem." Mr. Drake coughed meaningfully. "We do encourage all the children to speak English all the time," he said. Jai's mother flushed slightly and she repeated her words in English. Nervousness made her accent more pronounced.

"Now, now," Mr. Drake said cheerfully. "No need for sentimentality. Jai's going to have the time of his life here with the other boys and girls. And in next to no time Mother and Father will be back again."

It was exactly what they all hoped and dreamed of, so no one disagreed with Mr. Drake, even though Jai couldn't help feeling there was a false note in the headmaster's voice.

Jai kissed his mother one last time and watched her get into the car. He waved as the car drove slowly around the gravel circle and down the driveway. Then the hissing sound of the engine could no longer be heard.

"So, Jai," Mr. Drake said, "here you are at Nexhoath. Now come and meet our matron, Mrs. Frumbose." He stalked up the steps, leaving Jai to pick up his suitcase and struggle after him.

TWO

Inside the house looked both grand and decaying at the same time. The floor of the large entrance hall was of polished wood; old Persian rugs with frayed, curled edges were scattered here and there. An imposing staircase led upward. It was made of polished wood, too, with a gleaming balustrade, and brass rods holding down the carpet, which was also rather worn.

On the walls around the stairwell hung many gold-framed portraits of people in old-fashioned clothes. They had stiff faces and alarming eyes. Several of them wore the medals of Bureaucrats of the highest level. On the right of the front door hung the largest portrait of all. It looked unfinished, with dark patches on it like shadows, from which the finished parts stood out in an astonishingly life-like way. At first glance Jai thought it was of the headmaster, Mr. Drake, but then he wasn't so sure. There was something broken up about it, like a jigsaw puzzle that had not been put together properly. It gave him a headache.

He looked upward. An enormous chandelier was suspended from the ceiling. Its crystal pendants were supposed to reflect the light of a hundred little lamps, but the candles were not lit and the crystal was dusty.

The hall smelled dusty, too, beneath a faint aroma of beeswax polish and another smell that Jai couldn't identify. It tickled his nose and made him want to sneeze. He tried to sniff quietly. He didn't want to take out his handkerchief in case Mr. Drake thought he was crying.

To the right of the staircase was a huge wooden chest. Its sides gleamed with a dark patina as though it had once been well cared for, but its lid had warped and cracked with age. Above it hung a system of voice pipes, and a bell rope that Mr. Drake now pulled. Away in the distance Jai heard a bell ring faintly and again he thought he heard a dog barking. He remembered the glowing green eyes he'd seen in the hall.

"Do you have a dog?" he asked. He was not fond of dogs, especially not big ones.

"Certainly not," Mr. Drake replied. "I dislike all animals. And of course some of the children suffer from asthma. We have to be very aware of allergies." As he spoke he ran his hand over the surface of the chest and looked at his fingertips with a frown. He dusted them off on his coattails and tapped them together impatiently. The bell rope had drawn no response. Mr. Drake spoke into the voice pipe.

"Mrs. Frumbose, this is the headmaster speaking. Please come at once to the entrance hall."

His voice echoed distortedly through the pipe. At the end of the hall a door opened, and a woman stepped into the room. She was rather small and dumpy, with a round, neat face and bright yellowish eyes. Her hands were plump and soft, but the nails were long and sharp. She was wearing a dark gray quilted skirt and a light gray fluffy sweater under a spotlessly clean white apron. She had very small feet encased in shiny black shoes and white socks.

"Kitty," Mr. Drake said, in some surprise. "Where is Mrs. Frumbose?"

"Mrs. Frumbose's not feeling her best," Kitty replied, giving Jai a small smile. "She's got one of her headaches."

Mr. Drake frowned even more. His smooth face was growing craggy with annoyance. "I suppose you'll have to take over," he said, not sounding very pleased by the idea. "Can you manage?"

"Of course." Kitty had an unusual voice, slightly discordant, like a badly tuned violin. It made everything she said to Mr. Drake sound as if she were cross with him.

"This is Jai Kala," Mr. Drake said.

Kitty stared at Jai. Her gaze was so direct and inquisitive that he couldn't help returning it. She seemed to be trying to find out all about him just by staring. He wondered what she saw.

"Show Jai where he's sleeping." Mr. Drake looked at his fingertips again and frowned. "These old houses," he muttered. "They're impossible to keep clean."

"We do our best," Kitty said offhandedly. "We can't help it if we're understaffed." She turned to Jai and placed her little sharp-nailed hand gently on his arm. "Come along, dear. Give me that case; it's too heavy for you."

She led Jai through the door at the end of the hall and up two flights of a narrow staircase.

"Tiresome man," she muttered at the top landing. "There's nothing wrong with being clean. Goodness knows I'm very clean myself. But he makes a religion out of it."

She opened a door halfway along the landing. "There's a spare cubicle in this dormitory for you. I'll send some children up to help you unpack and show you around."

Jai was trying to remember the sequence of prime numbers. What came after thirty-seven? He was thinking about numbers because the smell of the staircase and the landing was so sad and depressing, like old boiled cabbage and sour milk. And the room Kitty had led him into was rather depressing, too, like a stable for horses with lots of cubicles looking just like stalls. Each one had an iron bed with a white counterpane on it, and a skimpy curtain across the front. There were eight of them. It dawned on him that he was going to have to sleep in this room with seven strangers.

He remembered the children he'd met—well, almost met—in the driveway. He hoped they might be in this dormitory, too.

"I met some children before," he said, and took the bone ring out of his pocket.

He was going to tell Kitty he'd found it, but he was silenced by her reaction. As soon as she saw the ring her eyes glassed over with surprise. The pupils opened up to huge black circles. Her mouth gaped, and she almost hissed at him.

"Put it away. Don't show it to anyone. No one must know it's here."

She put out a hand as if she were going to stroke Jai, as if she couldn't help touching him. Then she spoke as if to herself, in disjointed sentences that he didn't understand at all.

"To the very day! The day the Cat's Eye rises. And bearing the ring!"

She was shaking, her face glowing with delight. She smiled at Jai, showing pointed teeth. She picked up the suitcase that she had put on the floor and took him by the arm.

"I think one of the other rooms would be better for you," she said, her voice deep and husky. She led Jai out of the dormitory along the depressing passage, down one level of stairs and through a small door.

They emerged onto the landing at the top of the grand staircase. Jai sniffed appreciatively. Here everything smelled again of beeswax, with a trace of jasmine, rather like his own home. Kitty opened one of the doors onto the landing, and Jai walked into a very grand bedroom.

It had low windows looking out over the park. The mist had turned into rain, and the raindrops ran down the panes. Outside it was almost dark. Kitty put the suitcase on the floor and lit the lamp. It had an apricot-colored shade and deep cream fringe. The light gave the room a warm glow, and in fact, despite the winter and the late afternoon, it was not cold. A radiator gurgled and moaned in the corner, giving out a welcome heat.

There was only one bed in the room, a huge old four-poster. Jai sat down on it and was nearly swallowed up by the soft quilts and mattress.

"My mother said I'd have to sleep in a dormitory, with other children," he said shyly. The room was nice, but it was awfully grand and he thought later on it might seem awfully . . .

"You think you'll be lonely?" Kitty said, reading his thoughts. "But Roughly or I will keep an eye on you. If you need anything you only have to call, or ring the bell."

It didn't sound at all like what his parents had said. Jai tried to remember everything they'd told him about Nexhoath. *Like an English boarding school,* his father had said. He admired everything English extravagantly. *You're a lucky fellow.* And his mother had warned him, *It won't be like anything you're used to. But there'll be a lot of other children. You'll make lots of friends.* But here he was in this luxurious room, with no sign of any other children. If it hadn't been for the girl and boy in the driveway, he wouldn't have known there were other children here at all.

"You'll meet them soon," Kitty said, reading his thoughts again. She really had a strange voice, plaintive and squeaky. "Do you want to join them for supper downstairs, or would you rather I brought you a tray in your room?"

Jai stared at her. Once he and his parents had stayed in a very smart hotel, and he had been allowed to order from room service. A waiter had brought the most elegant sandwich he'd ever seen, along with equally elegant fried potatoes, on a silver tray. And yet the waiter had somehow known that they weren't the sort of people who usually stayed in hotels like that, and his face and voice had been very slightly scornful. There was nothing scornful about Kitty. She was waiting to see what he wanted, and whatever he wanted she would do. He wondered if she was like that with all the children. There was something creepy about her, something strange in the way she looked at him.

"I think I'd like to eat downstairs," he said. "With the others."

Her smile widened. "Of course," she said again. "I'll send someone to your room to fetch you when it's ready. If you don't mind, I must go and start cooking."

She made a slight movement, almost as if she were going to curtsy, and smiled even more broadly. "I'm so, so happy you're here," she said, then looked round sharply. "But I mustn't say anymore." She closed the door soundlessly.

Jai lay back on the pillows and looked up. Above his head the top of the four-poster bed sagged, just as if something were lying on it. It looked quite interesting now, while the light was on, the sort of thing you could make up a story about, but he was afraid it would look scary later. He would ask Kitty to take him to the dormitory. No matter what the other children were like, at least he wouldn't be on his own. Though Kitty had said she would be nearby. She or Roughly. Who on earth was Roughly? Another servant? One of the teachers?

The rain dripped steadily down the windowpanes. The radiator hissed gently. The lamp flickered. It seemed like a very long time since his mother had woken him that morning, since they had set off in the car, leaving the house in the city behind. Jai closed his eyes. He could feel himself drifting into sleep.

THREE

Jai was awakened about half an hour later by a tap on the door. He didn't know where he was. It took him a few moments to remember he was at Nexhoath, at boarding school. He had been dreaming something pleasant and he closed his eyes again, hoping to drift back into the dream.

But the tap came again, more insistently. There was a scuffle outside the door, the sound of voices raised in a brief argument. Then the door flew open. Jai sat straight up in surprise. Two children burst into the room, a boy and a girl, both wearing red sweaters. The boy was also wearing mossy green trousers, the girl blue stockings full of darns and patches.

They were the two children from the driveway. Jai stared at them.

They stared back at him. "Hello," the boy said. He was tall and well built, his thick fair hair nearly hiding blue-gray eyes. "We've come to bring you down for supper. I'm Hugo Martinez Fairweather, and this is Celia Abbott, but you have to call her Seal."

"Celia is a stupid name," the girl said. "And, anyway, nobody knows if it's my real name or not. It's just what *she* chose to call me. And *she* always pronounced it Seeeliaah. And *she* only said it when I did something she didn't like. Which was all the time." She didn't explain more, but gazed in awe around the room. "I've never been in one of these rooms before. They're normally out of bounds for us. Only Mr. Drake is allowed on this floor, except for the cleaners, of course." She turned to stare again at Jai. "Why did they put you in here? Are you someone special?" she demanded. "Are you a prince or something?"

"There haven't been any princes for a while," Hugo said. "The last one had to go home when his father died. I suppose he turned into a king. But even he didn't sleep in here."

They both looked at Jai accusingly, as if waiting for him to explain himself.

"A woman put me here," he said. "Kitty, her name is. I didn't know I wasn't supposed to be here. And, anyway, I'm not staying here. I'm going to sleep in the dormitory."

"Kitty is a very strange person," Seal observed. "Don't you think so, Hugo?"

"Not as strange as Mrs. Frumbose," Hugo said, sitting down on the end of the bed. "Mrs. Frumbose is the matron," he told Jai. "She's always having headaches and she cries a lot."

"It's the change of life," Seal said wisely. "My aunt's going through it, too. Mrs. Frumbose drinks, though, and my aunt doesn't. I don't know if that makes it better or worse. But Kitty is strange in a completely different way. Mrs.

Frumbose is straightforward mad. Kitty is . . . weird! Look at the way she speaks—almost as if she's yowling."

"I thought she was nice," Jai said.

They both looked at him. Was it with pity or scorn?

"Well, obviously you're going to be a favorite," Seal muttered.

"Adults at Nexhoath are not nice," Hugo explained. "Whether they're servants or teachers, doesn't matter, none of them is nice. At Nexhoath they are all the enemy."

"And the biggest enemy is Mr. Drake!" Seal added.

"Mr. Drake is a fiend," Hugo chanted.

"Mr. Drake is a drackle!"

"He's a cannibal drackle. He devours people."

"Especially new boys!"

"But he can't devour you if you're wearing red," Hugo leaned forward and whispered to Jai. "That's why Seal and me always wear our red sweaters. These are our special sweaters, knitted by my mother out of Patagonian wool and dyed with secret herbal dyes."

Seal stroked her sweater as if it was a pet cat. "Feel it. Lovely and soft, isn't it? Not like horrible scratchy school sweaters. Do you have anything red to wear? And what's your name, by the way?"

Jai looked at them warily. He wasn't sure if they were teasing him or not. They were quite unlike the boys at his old school, who tended either to thump you or ignore you. These two seemed to be playing some sort of elaborate game. He didn't understand it, but he thought it could be fun to be a part of.

"You're supposed to wear the school uniform, aren't you?" he said slowly, thinking of his brand-new uniform packed in the suitcase, his name embroidered on the inside of each garment by his mother.

"It's a funny thing," Seal said. "You don't *have* to wear the school uniform. I mean, it's not in the rules or anything. Hugo read the prospectus—what did it say, Hugo?"

"'School uniform optional,'" Hugo said. "That means you can choose whether to wear it or not. Before Mr. Drake came to be headmaster, no one used to wear it much at all."

"But since he arrived, sooner or later everyone seems to choose to wear it," Seal said. "Not us, though. We're the resistance. The rebels. The guerrillas."

"Lots of people started out as rebels," Hugo added, "and then slowly they began to appear in school uniform. It was just one or two at first—now it's almost one every day. There are hardly any guerrillas left."

Jai wondered if Hugo and Seal had been being guerrillas in the park that afternoon. He said, "I saw you earlier. My father nearly ran over you."

"We'd been up at the Clumps," Seal said. She took Jai to the window and pointed away up the hill. "It's too dark to see now, but they're up there. They're our special place. No one else goes there. It's out-of-bounds, really, so don't tell on us."

"You dropped something," Jai told her, taking the bone ring out of his pocket.

Seal fell on it with a shout of delight. "Thank goodness you found it! I thought I'd lost it." She put her thumb on the blank patch of the animal's face just as Jai had done earlier.

"What is it?" Jai asked.

"It's my most precious possession. It's the only thing I have that's always been mine. I'm an orphan, you see. That's why I have to live at Nexhoath." She slipped the ring into her pocket and grinned at Jai. He was not sorry to see the ring disappear. He didn't like the half-animal face. There was something disturbing about it.

"Why are you here?" Hugo asked.

Before Jai could answer, they heard from below the faint sound of a bell ringing.

"Time for supper!" Hugo said. "I'm starving."

Seal jumped off the bed. "Come on," she said to Jai. "We'd better take you down. What *is* your name?"

"Jai," he replied.

FOUR

Jai followed Seal and Hugo along the landing, away from the grand staircase. Apart from the room they had just left, all the doors were shut. At the end of the landing was the smaller door, almost like a cupboard, through which Jai had come with Kitty. Seal pulled it open, and they stepped through it.

"These are the back stairs," Hugo explained. He pointed upward. "That way leads up to the dorms. And down below are the dining room and the classrooms."

Not only the smell of the house changed on the other side of the door. The carpet was replaced by a rough corded floor covering. The wood of the staircase was not polished, but painted in thick, chipped dark brown paint. The light was a single faint gas jet. After the warmth of the bedroom, it felt chilly and dank. Jai couldn't help shivering as he went carefully down the stairs.

Seal and Hugo leaped down two at a time, despite the darkness. They waited at the bottom in a narrow passageway that led from the dining room to the kitchen. At the kitchen end was a swinging green baize door. Just as Jai stepped off the bottom stair and onto the linoleum-covered floor, the door swung open, and a man in a white apron stepped through carrying a dish of food in each hand.

"Oh," Hugo said, sniffing, "it's macaroni and cheese again."

"I love macaroni and cheese," Seal said.

"I love anything," Hugo said, "I'm so hungry."

As the man approached them the light hit his eyes. For a moment they gleamed green. He gave Jai a quick, fierce look, and his nose wrinkled very slightly. Then his face softened a little, almost as if he was going to smile. He gave a half nod and went on toward the dining room. They heard the sound of voices increase as the door opened, and a groan go up at the arrival of the macaroni and cheese.

"And then there's Roughly," Seal said, as if she were continuing the conversation from the bedroom. "Roughly is definitely very strange."

"Roughly likes Jai, too," Hugo said. "Did you notice he almost smiled?"

"Roughly never smiles," Seal told Jai. "He has some mysterious tragedy that's blighted his life. But Hugo's right. He did look as if he was going to smile." She peered at Jai through the darkness. "There must be something special about you."

"Who is Roughly?" Jai said. He didn't want to be special. He wanted to be just like all the other children and not stand out in any way. At Sherbrooke he had stood out too much, not only because of being Indian, but because of the way his parents treated him, as if he were made of glass, which he knew was quite different from the way most of the boys' parents acted. He'd always longed for his parents to be more casual, more rough-and-ready, so he would fit in better.

"Actually," Seal said, as though the idea had only just occurred to her, "no one's quite sure who Roughly is."

"He wasn't here last term," Hugo said. "He just turned up a few weeks ago. At the same time as Kitty, I might add."

"Perhaps he's her secret lover," Seal said, and giggled.

"Or her bodyguard," Hugo suggested.

"She's on the run from someone."

"They're bank robbers."

"And it's all got something to do with Jai."

"No it hasn't," Jai interrupted.

"Come on, let's go and eat," Hugo said.

In earlier days when Nexhoath was a private mansion it had a magnificent ballroom, which was now the school dining room, directly underneath the grand bedrooms where Jai had taken his afternoon nap. Floor-to-ceiling French windows opened onto a paved terrace, decorated with statues of draped ladies and urns holding dead plants. It was dark outside, and the eating children were reflected in the windows, so that beyond the terrace Jai could see nothing. The darkness and the rain beating on the windows made him feel as if he were on a ship at sea, just as his parents would be soon—though he'd never been on a ship, so he didn't know if that was what it really felt like. But there was something about the house that suggested sailing away from the everyday world, toward an unimaginable adventure.

"Wake up!" Seal said in his ear. "If you don't hurry, there'll be nothing left to eat."

Hugo had already pushed ahead to a table in the center of the room where Kitty stood, ladle in hand, serving children as fast as she could. Every now and then she would glance around the room, watchfully, and when she saw Jai in the line, her face relaxed and she made a little noise like a purr.

"You like macaroni and cheese?" she said when it was his turn to be served.

"I don't think I've ever tasted it," he replied.

"If you don't like it we'll find you something else," she said.

Hugo had saved seats for them. Seal's face was contorted in amazement as they sat down. "I've never heard that before," she said. "It's always, *Eat what's put in front of you, don't be so fussy, think of all the starving children in the world. . . .*" She looked suspiciously at Jai again. "Who are you really?" she said.

"I'm no one," he said stubbornly. "I just had to come here because my parents aren't allowed to live in this country anymore. . . ." He stopped abruptly. Saying it aloud made him gulp unexpectedly. He was going to explain, but now it seemed that it wasn't words waiting to come out of him, it was tears.

Seal took pity on him and said breezily, "Hugo's here

because his parents work in a place where there aren't any schools at all. It takes weeks and weeks just to get there, so he doesn't even go home for holidays."

"In South America," Hugo said, "right at the very, very bottom of Argentina. I was born there—that's why I'm called Martinez. It's my mother's name. I lived there till last year. It's the best place in the world, *el más hermoso país del mundo.*"

One of the teachers at the end of the table tapped his glass with his fork. "English only, Hugo!"

Hugo made a face at Seal surreptitiously and went on as if he hadn't heard. "I'm going back to live there just as soon as I've finished being educated.

"And Seal's here because . . ." Hugo stopped and looked at the girl sitting on the other side of Jai. "Do you want to tell him?"

"It's no big deal," she said, although she frowned as though perhaps it was. Her hand went into her pocket. Jai guessed she had her fingers on the bone ring. He could almost feel the smooth cold bone under his own thumb.

"My parents died when I was a baby," Seal said in a sad but dramatic voice. "I don't remember them at all. I used to live with someone—she said she was my aunt, but I don't believe she was any relation. No one of my own blood could be so nasty. She's the one who called me Seeeliaah. I hated living with her, and she hated having me there, so one day, after a really huge fight, I ran away. The police came after me and took me back. She said she couldn't control me anymore, and I had to come to boarding school. And that was exactly a year ago today. I've been at Nexhoath for one whole year and I've never been home. My aunt said I've got to stay at boarding school until I'm old enough to earn my own living."

"Won't that be a terribly long time away?" Jai asked.

"Years and years, probably. Nexhoath only takes children up to eighth grade. I don't know where I'll go when I leave here."

"You could always run away again," Hugo suggested through a mouthful of macaroni and cheese.

"I would if you'd come with me. I only stay because you're here." Seal held the ring up to her cheek.

"Put it away," Hugo said. "If the teachers see it, they'll confiscate it."

Seal slid the ring into her pocket, looking around anxiously.

"See, we're best friends," Hugo said. "We look out for each other."

Jai took a forkful of macaroni and cheese. It was milky and slimy, and the cheese smelled faintly sour. His stomach closed. He managed to force down the mouthful he'd taken, but he couldn't face another one. He put his fork down.

"Aren't you going to eat it?" Seal said in surprise. She took the plate and began to divide Jai's meal between herself and Hugo.

"First rule of boarding school," Hugo said. "You eat

whenever you can, because you're always hungry."

Jai felt as if he would never be hungry again in his life. Watching the other two polish off his food made him feel slightly sick. He turned away and inspected the room.

Most of the children were too busy eating to take any notice of him. There were about fifty of them sitting at five long tables, ten to a table. Though they were obviously of various nationalities, they had an air of sameness about them, with their smooth, clean faces, neat hair, and eyes that gave nothing away. One or two of them glanced at Jai, but no one showed any real curiosity about him, and no one spoke to him. No one spoke much at all. They ate in a serious, orderly fashion, sitting politely in their places.

Each table had a teacher sitting at the head. There were three women and two men. They all wore severe black clothes, like Mr. Drake, though the women wore skirts instead of trousers. None of them looked very comfortable. They shifted their shoulders inside their jackets, and scratched their necks where the coarse worsted material rubbed against their skin. They all had bland faces, and their eyes were cold.

Most of the children were wearing navy blue sailor suits with either shorts or skirts, which Jai knew were part of the school uniform. Only a few were wearing their own home clothes, standing out in patches of color. Jai counted them for something to do. There were five including Hugo and Seal—three girls and two boys. Six if he counted himself.

He studied these children. It was not only the clothes that made them look different. Their faces were more lively, and unlike the others they laughed sometimes. One girl in particular attracted his attention. She reminded him a little of his mother. She had the same fine features and dark hair and eyes. She was wearing a deep purple sweater, and she had little gold earrings. When she saw Jai staring at her, she made a face at him and then grinned.

She nudged the boy next to her in the ribs. He was wearing a bright blue vest over a shirt of fine white wool. He turned and stared at Jai, too.

Jai looked away, embarrassed. He found himself watching Roughly instead.

Roughly stood motionless at the door that led to the passage. Jai tried to watch him secretly, but it was impossible. As soon as he looked in Roughly's direction, the man swung his shaggy head toward him, and their eyes met. Roughly's hair was coarse, darkish, streaked with gray, and he had a long nose and big teeth. His hands were big, with short stubby fingers, and strong, square nails. His eyes were deep-set and rather mournful. It was hard to see what color they were.

Kitty circled the room noiselessly, keeping a watchful eye on the children. Nothing went on in the dining room that Kitty didn't notice. But her gaze always returned to Jai.

Suddenly one of the teachers rang a handbell. Everyone stopped eating and jumped to their feet. Hugo nudged Jai.

"That's Mr. Porteous. He's the deputy headmaster. He used to be the head until Mr. Drake came, and he was much nicer then, too."

Mr. Porteous was younger than Mr. Drake. His face was brown, as if he spent much of his time out-of-doors, but it was perfectly still and controlled. He looked around the room, waiting for silence. Then he spoke in a calm, expressionless voice. "We will say the Nexhoath words together."

The children all began to speak in unison. "We are proud to belong to Nexhoath, glad to respect and obey our teachers, and thankful for our food."

"Dada da dah!" The boy with the white shirt and blue vest beat out a cheeky rhythm on the table and made a flamboyant gesture. The dark girl next to him laughed and put in some dance steps as if she were tap-dancing.

Mr. Porteous glared at them. The dining room fell silent.

"Jamie? Sunita? Is there something you wish to share with the rest of us?"

Jamie shook his head, saying nothing, trying to stifle giggles. Sunita said in a clear voice, "I am not proud to belong and I am not thankful for that food."

"Jamie, Mr. Drake wants to see you after supper. Sunita, come to me in my study later. Everyone else dismissed."

The children left quietly in neat lines. Jai followed Hugo and Seal. So the girl in the purple sweater was called Sunita. He hoped she wasn't going to get into trouble.

FIVE

After supper the children went upstairs to their sitting rooms and were allowed to play games or read books until bedtime. Seal and Hugo undertook to give Jai a tour of the house. The fifty children were divided, according to age, into four classes, and each class had roughly one quarter of the huge old house. Classrooms were on the ground floor, and sitting rooms and dormitories on the third floor.

"This is where you'd sleep," Hugo said, opening the door to the dormitory.

"I know," Jai replied. "Kitty showed me before."

"I'd stay in the room you're in if I were you," Seal said, kicking off her shoes and sliding down the linoleum that ran through the middle of the dormitory. "It looks a lot more comfy, and it's much warmer."

The dormitory was definitely chilly. Jai could see his own breath in the air. "Primitive, isn't it?" Hugo said. "Never mind. You'll get used to it. This is my cubicle, here."

Jai admired the pictures on the walls, the miniatures of Hugo's mother and little sisters in their Argentinean home, and the sketch of his father, wearing leather chaps and riding a horse.

Seal's cubicle was opposite on the girls' side of the dormitory. She had no family pictures, but on the wall above her bed were several drawings of birds and insects and a pencil sketch of three horses.

"I love animals," Seal explained. "I like studying them and trying to draw them. This is a swallow that flew into the dorm last summer and sat on the curtain rod for ages. And this is a praying mantis. I kept it in my drawer for a while. The horses live in the paddock. I did that picture when Miss Arkady first came to the school. She was nice for about a week, before Mr. Drake got to her. Now she never lets me draw horses."

The cubicle nearest the door on the boys' side was unoccupied. "You could go in here," Hugo said. "Jean-Michel was here, but he didn't come back this term."

"The whole family went back to France," Seal informed him. "Some ancient relative died, and they inherited a title and a château. Jean-Michel is now the Duc de Guisnes."

Jai looked at the narrow space, the iron bed, the washbasin, and jug. It was a lot more spartan than the luxurious room Kitty had put him in. But he didn't want to leave Hugo and Seal, especially as night had now come completely down over the house, isolating it in an ocean of darkness.

"If I could find Kitty," he said, "I could move my things in here."

"Let's go look for her," Hugo said, leading the way.

Just outside the dormitory door a narrow stairway led

upward. The farther up the house you went, the smaller the stairways became. There was a notice on the wall above the first step: PRIVATE. NO ENTRY.

"That's the way up to the servants' quarters and the matron's apartment," Hugo said. "There's a sickroom up there, too. I went there when I had tonsillitis last year. It's so high up. The view's wonderful; you can see right across the valley. I wouldn't have minded being there, but Mrs. Frumbose was being really vile. So I got better in a hurry. Anyway, Seal was pining, so I couldn't stay away any longer."

"You know I can't survive without you," she said.

From upstairs came the sound of a door opening and closing, followed by the soft tread of feet. Kitty appeared around the curve of the little staircase, her eyes gleaming in the half light.

"Kitty, Kitty," Seal said when she saw her, "Jai wants to move into the dormitory. Can we get his things?"

Kitty stared at each of them in turn with her amber eyes. Then she smiled slightly and said to Jai, "You may certainly move if you wish. Roughly will bring your suitcase over immediately."

Seal gave Hugo a nudge.

"You can help him unpack," Kitty said to them sharply.

"We will." Seal nodded. When Kitty had padded down the stairs to the kitchen, Seal whispered, "Let's go and help Roughly. I want to see that part of the house again."

They raced down and found Roughly on his way up. He

nodded and smiled at Jai and spoke to him in a deep gruff voice. "Just going to get your luggage."

Seal dug Jai in the back. "Ask him," she hissed.

"Um, can we come, too?" Jai asked.

Roughly gave him a look almost of surprise. "You can do whatever you like," he said. "You only have to ask."

Hugo thought about this for a couple of moments as they all went back to the second floor. "What about us?" he said. "Can we do whatever we like, too?"

"No," Roughly replied, and said no more.

The three children followed him through the door and onto the main landing. Immediately the different smell of the grand part of the house enveloped them, and they all breathed in deeply. Roughly went on to the bedroom while they stayed on the landing, looking around.

"Mmmm." Seal sighed. "Isn't it heavenly! I wish I could stay on this side."

"With the Dead Baby?" Hugo said.

"Don't remind me, Hugo! I'd forgotten the Dead Baby. You're right! I guess I wouldn't dare stay here on my own." She leaned over the balustrade and pointed downward. "See the chest there?" she said to Jai, "with the big crack in the lid?"

Jai looked over the edge, past the dusty chandelier. He remembered noticing the chest when Mr. Drake had pulled the bell rope. Had it really been only that afternoon? It felt like a lifetime ago.

"That's where the Dead Baby was found," Seal whispered in his ear. "The nurse put a baby in there to hide it while she was meeting her boyfriend, and they forgot about it, and when the mother opened the chest the baby was dead, and the mother screamed so loud, the lid cracked. The baby cries in the night, and you see its little hands pushing up through the crack. . . ."

Jai felt all the hair on the back of his neck stand up in fright. Now he was even more glad he wasn't staying in the grand room so close to the hall and the chest. "Is that true?" he asked nervously.

"Of course, it's true," Hugo said. "The mother went mad, and the family sold the house. That's why it's a boarding school now."

Jai looked from Hugo to Seal and back again. It was like their story about Mr. Drake being a cannibal drackle. There was no way of knowing if they were playing a game or not. He was about to question them further when he heard a door opening below.

"Someone's coming," Seal said.

They all ducked down and peered through the carved rails. The boy in the bright blue vest, Jamie, came slowly into the hall from the direction of the kitchen. He looked a little anxiously at the Dead Baby chest, then knocked on the door of Mr. Drake's study.

The door opened. Mr. Drake stepped out into the hall. From above he appeared particularly old. His hair looked thin and gray, and he was stooped. His voice sounded old and creaky, too.

"Ah, Jamie," they heard him say. "I just wanted to have a little chat with you about your future." Then the door closed, and they could hear nothing from inside.

Instead they heard a strange noise from behind them. Roughly had returned from the bedroom, carrying Jai's suitcase. He was staring at the closed door, his eyes blazing with anger, his mouth open in a half snarl.

SIX

Roughly carried the suitcase back to the dormitory, and Seal and Hugo helped Jai put his things away. With a squeal of delight Seal held up the red pajamas that Jai's mother had bought him for his birthday.

"Put them on," she said. "Then you'll be safe from Mr. Drake!"

"He can't wear pajamas all the time," Hugo pointed out. "Don't you have anything else red?"

But Jai had only the pajamas.

"You don't really have to wear red, do you?" he asked, still not sure if Hugo and Seal were teasing him or not.

"It's worked so far, hasn't it?" Hugo replied, shoving a handful of socks into the chest of drawers.

"This is nice," Seal said, holding up Jai's favorite shirt. It was gray-and-white-checked wool, handspun, with a gray hood and pockets. "Wear this and you'll be safe, even if it's not red."

The door opened, and they all looked up. Jamie came into the dormitory. He gave them a nod, went into his cubicle, two down from Hugo's, and drew the curtain without speaking to them.

Hugo and Seal exchanged a look.

"Hey, Jamie," Hugo called. "What did the old drackle say to you?"

"You shouldn't speak about Mr. Drake like that," Jamie said quietly and clearly. "He was just giving me some advice, that's all."

Seal put the last of Jai's clothes into a drawer. Her high spirits had suddenly disappeared. She was biting her lip.

"Bet he's in school uniform tomorrow," Hugo whispered.

"What do you mean?" Jai said, looking from one to the other. "What's going on?"

"You'll be all right," Seal said, with a touch of envy. "Everyone's looking after you. Even if you won't tell us why." She stood up. "But who's going to look after me?" she said. "And who's going to look after Hugo?"

"We'll look after each other, like we always do," Hugo said cheerfully. "And I think it's time we made a plan of action."

A bell rang in the distance, and a distorted voice spoke through the voice pipe. "All children to their dormitories. Lights out in fifteen minutes."

"What can we do?" Seal asked. "You see what Mr. Drake's like. He gets everyone in the end."

"I've got a bit of an idea," Hugo replied. "I need to think about it some more. Let's have a Council of War tomorrow."

"At the Clumps after school?" Seal's eyes brightened. Hugo nodded.

Seal gestured at Jai. "What about him?"

"I think he's important," Hugo answered. "He's got a

hold over Kitty and Roughly. That could be useful."

"Did you notice how angry Roughly was before?" Seal said to Hugo. "He must hate Mr. Drake almost as much as we do. Do you think there's a chance he'd be on our side?" She turned eagerly to Jai. "Are you going to be one of us?" she demanded.

Jai gazed at her, not knowing what to reply. Suddenly he was achingly tired. He didn't want to think about anything else. He just wanted to be asleep.

Kitty appeared like magic in the doorway. "Time for bed," she said to the children. Compared to the disembodied voice from the voice pipe, she sounded friendly and kind.

Other children came into the dormitory and began to get ready for bed. Jai brushed his teeth and put on his red pajamas. He slipped between the sheets. They were rough and slightly damp, and the covers were not very heavy. He thought about everything that had happened on this long, strange day. He was cold, a little hungry, and just the tiniest bit homesick. He turned his mind to numbers and started to do a very complicated long-division sum in his head, but he was too tired to stay awake for long. Just before he fell asleep he thought he heard a dog barking, but then it turned into a dream.

The next morning he had to learn the school routine. At six-thirty a bell rang for everyone to get up, and breakfast was at seven. After breakfast the children had to make their beds and clean the dormitories and bathrooms, and then everyone went out on the terrace for morning exercises. Mr. Porteous, in hemp shorts and leather mountaineering boots, took some of the children for a run around the park. Hugo went with him. Seal and Jai stayed on the terrace and did a lot of stretches, jumping jacks, and jogging on the spot with Miss Arkady.

The rain had stopped, and a pale wintry sun was breaking up the mist. The heads of the old horses, who were used to pull the grass cutter and the drays, loomed through the haze like pieces from a huge chess game.

"Aren't they beautiful?" Seal said, jumping energetically next to Jai. "I love horses. I call the two grays Moonlight and Starlight, and the bay I call Midnight."

"Silence during exercise, Celia," snapped Miss Arkady. She was red in the face, puffing, and looked extremely uncomfortable in her neck-to-knee, tightly buttoned calico health outfit. "And one-two-three, and bend-two-three, and down-two-three, and up-two-three."

Seal scowled at her. "It's not hurting anyone if I talk," she said. "What difference does it make to you? I can talk while I exercise and still not get out of breath."

"You could talk and do anything," Sunita observed, jumping and stretching in the least energetic way possible. "You never stop talking."

"Me?" Seal retorted. "How about you, Sunita Chatterji? Chatter chatter, all day long."

"Girls, that's enough," Miss Arkady said loudly. "Fifty extra jumping jacks for you, Celia."

"What about Sunita?" Seal cried in outrage.

"Don't argue."

"Oh, that is so unfair," Seal wailed, tears springing into her eyes.

The first lesson was geography, with Mr. Drake. Mr. Drake came into the classroom looking fresh and young. Even his voice, as he told them about the Siberian tundra, was strong and loud. Then came math, with Mr. Corio; English, with Mrs. Antrobus, and morning recess when Kitty gave Jai specially baked muffins, which he shared with Seal and Hugo. After recess came science, with Mr. Porteous, followed by art, with Miss Arkady. By the time lunch arrived, the day had already seemed an endless whirl of bells ringing, disembodied voices giving orders, children rushing from one place to the next, and teachers teaching mainly incomprehensible subjects. Jai felt he would never catch up, never know where he was meant to be, and never get there on time with the right equipment.

At lunch he looked for Jamie, but couldn't recognize him. The children all looked so similar. He counted how many children were still wearing casual clothes. Now there were only four; five, including Jai himself. Sunita stood out in her purple sweater. She was in most of Jai's classes. He hoped he might become friends with her, even though she and Seal didn't seem to get along.

He was wearing gray trousers and the gray-and-white-checked top with a hood. But even in his favorite clothes he felt a little uncomfortable. There certainly was a lot of pressure at

Nexhoath to become like everyone else. The children stood at attention before and after every class to say "good morning" in unison to the teachers. Many of the lessons were learned by rote, and unless the children were repeating something, complete silence was the rule.

At recess Sunita and another girl brought out a length of stretchy cord and started playing a game, jumping in and out of it, but as soon as Mrs. Antrobus spotted them, she confiscated the cord, saying no one was allowed to bring new games into Nexhoath.

"That is so unfair," Seal whispered to him as they lined up for science. Jai agreed with her, but even though he liked Hugo and Seal and wanted to be friends with them, he didn't think he was cut out to be a rebel or a guerrilla. He thought he would probably start wearing the school uniform pretty soon. Thinking of the smart new school clothes that his mother had bought and named with so much care, it seemed a pity not to.

By the time lunch had ended he had decided to change into the sports uniform for games. But when he went up to the dormitory, Seal grabbed him at the doorway and pulled him into her cubicle.

"You've got to be on our side, Jai," she whispered. "You saw what happened to Jamie!"

"What *did* happen to him?"

"Mr. Drake got him. He's just like everyone else now. He's wearing the school uniform and everything and he's forgotten that he used to be anything different!"

"Seal . . . ," Jai began.

She held up a hand to silence him. "Don't argue! Just come to the Clumps with us. We'll talk about it there."

"We're supposed to join in, aren't we?" Jai said. "My parents said I had to make every effort to join in and make friends."

"I don't suppose they knew what sort of a place this was, though," Seal replied. "I bet they had to find somewhere for you in a hurry, and Nexhoath was the only choice."

Jai couldn't deny it. Seal gave him a pitying look and went on. "It's the same with everyone. And since Mr. Drake arrived, they all end up the same. He gets them all in the end. That's why you've absolutely got to help us."

"I don't know." Jai shrugged his shoulders. "I'm going to change into my sports uniform now."

"You can't," she said. "He'll get you, too! You think it's a game, don't you? But it's more than that. It's serious. It's real. Mr. Drake's doing something to all the children in the school, and we've got to stop him."

Her eyes were huge. No one had ever pleaded with Jai so intensely. He found it impossible to say no to her.

"All right," he agreed reluctantly. "I'll come this afternoon. But I don't know what I can do. I may as well warn you, I'm not a rebel or a guerrilla or anything like that."

"But you're special in some way, aren't you?"

"No," Jai almost shouted.

"Well, Kitty and Roughly think you are," Seal replied.

SEVEN

When Jai, Seal, and Hugo arrived on the sports field, Mr. Porteous was organizing everyone into groups to play soccer.

Jai found himself with Seal in what was obviously a B team, while Hugo played a fast and furious game with the more skillful players.

Jai quite liked sports, though he'd always been too small to get onto any of the teams at his old school, but today was not the sort of day when he felt like playing. The rain still held off, but the morning sun had disappeared and the air was raw. His ears and eyes ached from the cold, and the game was so frustrating. He had no idea who was on his side. Apart from Sunita, the girl she had been playing with at recess, and Seal, everyone was in the calico shorts and black jerseys, which were the sports uniform. They all looked so much the same that Jai kept passing to the wrong side. At times it seemed as though everyone was against him. They played fiercely and meanly, with no sense of fun or enjoyment, and with hardly any noise at all. By halftime he was bruised and panting. Seal had had several outbursts and had been sent off. She was sitting sulking on the paddock fence talking to the horses.

Jai felt too tired even to walk over to her. He collapsed

on a bench, next to Sunita. He'd noticed her during the game, looking different from the others in her white fur ear-muffs and gloves. She hardly played at all, just kept rather skillfully out of everyone's way. Every few minutes Miss Arkady had shouted at her, "Sunita, will you please join in?"

Each time Sunita had answered, "Certainly, Miss Arkady," and had carried on exactly the same as before, staying on the outskirts of the fray and doing dance steps to keep herself warm.

Now she grinned at Jai.

He smiled, still breathless.

"Do you get asthma?" she asked. Jai shook his head.

"That's a shame. I don't, either. If you did you could get excused from sports."

"I don't mind sports," Jai replied, finally able to speak.

"I think they're stupid," Sunita said. "People should not be made to run around outside in this sort of weather."

"I don't mind the running around," Jai replied, "but it's so hard to tell who's on which side."

Sunita looked at the other children. "They all look the same," she said. "Even Jamie, now. I don't want to be like that. Never do the same as everybody else, that's what my father says."

She said it with such a regal air that Jai wondered if her father was a king and she was a princess.

"Is that why you don't wear the school uniform?" he asked.

Sunita stroked the soft wool of her sweater. "The uniform is always scratching and itching," she said. "I like my clothes to feel good on me. I like to look different." Miss Arkady blew the whistle, and the game started again. Sunita stayed sitting on the bench until her name had been called at least four times. Then she arose languidly and went back to practicing her dance steps.

At the end of the game Jai found himself walking next to her as the children trooped back toward the house for afternoon tea. He was about to ask her more about herself, find out why she was at Nexhoath, when Seal ran up and pushed in between them.

Grabbing Jai, she pulled him aside and hissed into his ear, "Don't forget. The Council of War!"

Sunita shrugged her shoulders and walked on scornfully. Jai said to Seal, "Why don't we ask Sunita, too?"

"Her? No! I hate her! She's so stuck-up!"

"But she's not wearing the school uniform!"

"She'd give us away. I don't trust her."

Jai was about to argue when Hugo came hurrying toward them, holding out a paper bag. "Here, I ran ahead and got first in the line! We'll eat them on the way up to the Clumps!" He looked at Seal's face. "What's up now?"

"Jai wants to ask Sunita to come with us," Seal said, taking a fruit bun from the bag and biting into it.

"Well, we could," Hugo said slowly. "It's not a bad idea. Sunita's all right. She never does what anyone tells her. And we may need all the help we can get!"

"I don't want to ask her," Seal said loudly.

"You don't have to get upset. It's too late to ask her now anyway." Sunita had disappeared into the house along with all the other children. "But after I've told you my plan, we'll think about sounding her out, all right? Now let's hurry, we've only got a little while before prep begins."

At the back of the house was a jumble of outbuildings, stables, storehouses, and barns. Ducking behind these, Hugo led the way to a little footbridge over a stream. Instead of crossing it, they turned and followed the stream uphill.

At first it ran between the vegetable gardens, where channels had been dug for irrigation. Then it disappeared under the mill, making the wheel go clacking busily around. Beyond the mill the stream narrowed. The water rushed between slippery banks, over weeds that streamed like hair just below the surface. Then the slope steepened, the grass banks gave way to rocks, and the stream became more noisy as it chattered over the stones.

They climbed in silence. Jai wondered if he would make it to the top. His legs were already aching after the soccer game, and the fruit bun hadn't really filled the empty space in his stomach.

He was thinking that no matter what was for dinner he would eat every mouthful, when Hugo and Seal suddenly disappeared from view. He hurried after them and saw they had dropped down the bank and were crossing the stream, leaping from rock to rock. Jai followed them, his heart in his mouth. He thought suddenly about his parents. They would be surprised to see him now! He made it to the other side, but there was no chance to rest. Seal already had gone bounding up the side of the hill.

By following the stream they had come almost halfway to the Clumps, staying out of sight of the house. But it meant scaling the rest of the hill on the steepest slope. Jai had thought his legs hurt before—they felt as if they were going to collapse under him now. When the children reached the top and ran under the shelter of the trees, he fell to the ground as soon as the other two stopped.

Hugo was looking at his watch. "That's not bad," he said. "Twelve and a half minutes."

"Jai slowed us down a bit," Seal said, flopping down next to him.

Jai lay on his back gazing up at the branches of the pine trees. If he knew how far they had come in twelve and a half minutes he could have worked out how fast they'd been going. The pine needles below him were quite dry. The rain of the night before had not penetrated to them. They smelled strong and fresh. Above his head the wind soughed in the branches. "I don't know why we had to hike all the way up here. Why didn't we just talk back at the school?"

"This is a special place," Seal said. "No one can hear us.

We're safe here. We can talk without being spied on all the time."

"Get up," Hugo nudged Jai with his foot. "We must go farther in."

Jai reluctantly got to his feet and followed the other two deeper into the pine forest. They stopped in front of a semi-circle of rocks that looked almost as if it had been placed there on purpose. Scattered in front of the rocks were whitish objects. As Jai drew closer he could see they were bones. He shivered.

"It's creepy here. I don't like it."

"It's not creepy," Seal said. "We're safe here because the animals protect us. This is their place. This is where their bones lie. I climbed up here just after I first came to Nexhoath. At this time of year you can see the Cat's Eye from here. Once I'd seen the Cat's Eye, I knew I'd be all right."

Jai remembered Kitty had mentioned the Cat's Eye. "What is that?"

"It's the first star you see in the evening. At this time of year it rises in the east. We'll see it soon. It'll come up between those two rocks, just as the sun sets behind Nexhoath. They're all in a line, you see. That's why this is a magic place."

Jai couldn't deny that the place had a strong atmosphere of something, though he wasn't sure what. And he wasn't sure about animals protecting them, either. Surely animals were fierce and wild and likely to attack you for no reason at all? He noticed Seal had taken the bone ring out of her pocket. It was the same color as the bones on the ground, and could have been carved from one of them.

"What's your plan?" Seal asked Hugo.

Hugo took a deep breath. "Let's look at what happens. Mr. Drake calls people to his study. He says he wants to talk about their future. . . ."

"That's what headmasters do," Jai put in. "All the teachers did that at my last school."

Hugo ignored him. "And when they come out, they're changed in some way. They all wear the uniform, they all start to look the same. And they forget what he's done to them and how they used to be."

Seal shivered. "He really is a drackle. That's what drackles do. They steal something from you, your soul or your future."

"I want to find out what happens," Hugo went on. "There's only one way to do it. I'm going to see him. I'll put on the uniform and ask if I can have a talk with him. That way we'll find out what he's really up to."

"You can't do that! He'll take you over, too!" Seal protested.

"I hope he won't. I hope I'll be able to stop him. But if I can't stop him, you and Jai will have to. That's why I think we can do it now. Because Kitty and Roughly are looking after Jai, you can get them to help if we need anyone else."

"It's awfully dangerous," Seal said. "Why don't I do it?"

"He'll suspect something if it's you," Hugo replied. "But Mr. Porteous wants me to play on the soccer team, and I have to wear the uniform for that, so it'll all seem quite natural."

Seal stared at him. "You're not doing it because you want to be on the soccer team?"

"No, of course I'm not," Hugo said. "That just gives me a good reason. I've got to find out exactly what he does."

Seal was biting her lip. Jai shivered. He sat up and wrapped his arms around his chest. Half of him was glad and proud that Seal and Hugo wanted him to be part of their plan, but the other half kept trying to work out math in his head as if it was nothing to do with him at all.

He thought of what his parents had said about trying to fit in. But they hadn't known Mr. Drake was some kind of cannibal drackle. If he really was. Maybe he wasn't. Maybe it was just a game that Seal and Hugo believed in too much.

"You are going to help us, aren't you, Jai?" Seal said.

"What if it's not really true? What if he's not really a drackle?" Jai replied.

"Then I'll be in no danger at all," Hugo said, grinning. "And I can play on the soccer team and everything. But if we're right, and he is what we think he is, it's up to you two to stop me caving in completely. You'll have to watch through the window or something, all right? Create a diversion, stop him before it's too late."

Seal nodded abruptly. "I don't know what else we can do. We've got to find out what's going on." She held out the bone ring to Hugo. "You should have something that's not uniform," she said. "As long as you carry this, we'll know you're safe."

"I won't need it," Hugo protested, but Seal insisted until he took the ring.

As his fingers closed over it, the light that had been growing steadily darker seemed to brighten.

"Here it is," Seal said. "Here's the Cat's Eye."

A huge luminous star was rising between two of the rocks. True to its name, its light had an amber quality.

"Look," Hugo said, turning Jai to face the opposite direction.

The sun was setting behind Nexhoath. Golden light streamed through a break in the gray clouds. The old house stood out like a silhouette. For a moment Jai felt as if he was caught in a corridor of light.

"See," Hugo said. "We'll be all right. The cat has its eye on us. Now we'd better get back. Don't want to raise the drackle's suspicions."

He pulled Jai to his feet. "And if anything happens to me," he said, "tell Roughly. I've got an idea he hates Mr. Drake as much as we do."

EIGHT

Later that night Jai lay in bed, unable to sleep. Even reciting the one hundred times tables didn't calm him down. He thought of his parents. In a few days they would be on the ship. He had no idea how long their journey would take, but he knew it could be ages before he heard anything from them. He tried to imagine what they would say if they knew what was going on at Nexhoath. He suspected they would not believe any of it. And even if they believed it, they would not want him to make trouble. They knew that in the Bureaucracy it was better not to make a fuss, but to try and fit in, to try above all not to be noticed. That was what they had attempted to do for as long as he could remember and what they had told him to do all the time. But it hadn't helped them. They had hoped no one would notice them, but in the end the Bureaucracy had caught up with them. They hadn't had the right papers and so they were going to be deported. The injustice of it made him toss and turn. He felt like crying out, like Seal, *It isn't fair, it isn't fair!*

So what was the right thing to do now? To do what they had always told him to do, or to help Hugo and Seal?

He kept turning from one side to the other, his mind a

jumble of anxiety mixed with homesickness. The mattress was lumpy, and the pillow was itchy. The things Hugo and Seal had said kept echoing in his brain. And every time he was about to fall asleep he saw green eyes, glowing in the dark, watching him, watching him. . . .

He awoke with a start. There was something heavy on his feet. Heavy and soft and warm. . . .

An animal! He sat up and tried to pull his feet away. The animal turned its head, and he could see the shape of its ears, slightly darker than the darkness. It was a cat.

A cat was sitting on the end of the bed. Where on earth had it come from? Hadn't Mr. Drake said he disliked animals? Surely there weren't any animals at Nexhoath, apart from the horses in the paddock?

Jai wasn't sure if he liked animals or not. His parents had a great respect for them—his mother was even a vegetarian—but they had never had pets of any sort. Jai could remember his first visit to the zoo and his feeling of shock that all these creatures shared his world. Animals didn't seem controllable. They were always doing unexpected things, sometimes dangerous, sometimes disgusting. He lay down very quietly, holding his breath, hoping the cat would go away.

It didn't. It stretched a little and started to move toward him. Jai quickly pulled the bedclothes over his head.

With a swipe the cat whipped them off him. Its claws came so close that he felt the air move against his face.

"Get up, Jai," the cat yowled. "You've got to start lessons now."

This is a dream, Jai thought. *I don't remember falling asleep, but obviously I did, and now I'm dreaming about cats, because of Seal and Hugo going on about the Cat's Eye.*

This explanation was so satisfactory that he lay down again and closed his eyes.

The cat very gently stuck its claws into his knee.

Jai sat bolt upright, his eyes wide open.

"Get up," it yowled again.

It was looking at him very fiercely. There seemed to be nothing to do but obey. He got out of bed reluctantly and followed it out of the dormitory, up the narrow stairs that led to the servants' quarters and Mrs. Frumbose's flat at the top of the house. On one side of the landing several doors led off to different rooms, and on the other side three small windows opened out onto the roof. From behind Mrs. Frumbose's apartment door came a loud noise of snoring.

"Horrible, isn't it?" the cat said, pausing for a moment and flattening its ears. "It's because she drinks, you know. But it suits our purposes."

It padded softly across the linoleum to the middle window. "Open it," it said to Jai.

In a way that made him still think that he was dreaming, he did as the cat said, without question. The window was a small sash. He had to open the catch and raise the lower window frame. It was stiff, the cords were old, and he struggled for a few seconds. The cat meowed impatiently. Finally the window shot upward. The cold night air rushed in, making Jai shiver. The cat leaped nimbly through the window, then leaned in again, its front paws resting on the sill.

"Come on," it said to Jai.

He wasn't sure how to get out the window. It was too high to climb through, and he was afraid to leap like the cat had. Finally he heaved himself up and scrabbled over the windowsill, tumbling out on the other side onto the flat roof. The cat looked at him scornfully. "That wasn't very graceful," it said, shaking its head.

Jai picked himself up, rubbing his knees, which were damp from puddles that had collected on the roof. He looked around. He could see the whole top of the house. The sloping slates of the dormer roof were topped by a stone parapet that ran around the area where he was standing. Every few yards along the parapet a stone ornament— an urn or an eagle—rose majestically over the roof. Inside the parapet were several chimneys and one huge skylight, which Jai realized was directly above the main staircase of the house. Its edges were sealed by lead strips, and the glass was streaky and brown.

Several valleys sloped down from the center of the roof to take rainwater away, and old lead pipes linked them to gutters through the parapet. There were a lot of soggy dead leaves around, blocking the gutters in several places.

It was not raining, but the wind was gusty, and it whistled past his ears, making them ache with cold. Ragged clouds scudded across the sky, revealing then hiding a few stars and a quarter moon.

"There's so much you've got to learn," the cat said, studying him carefully. "It's hard to know where to start."

Its eyes glowed and then darkened as the moonlight came and went behind the racing clouds. "Balance," it said, "and lightness. Spring. Night vision." It purred slightly and walked delicately around Jai, rubbing its head against the back of his knees. "Let's try the window again."

The cat gathered all four paws neatly on the sill and then ran down the inside wall, landing soundlessly on the linoleum-covered floor.

"I can't do that!" Jai whispered. "I'm the wrong shape." But he watched the fluidity of the cat and tried to imitate it. After several attempts he found that by holding on to the sides of the window frame and swinging himself through he could land almost as silently. His bare feet padded on the linoleum. He became aware of how they touched the ground, how he could feel every part of the surface he was standing on, how it gave him push and spring.

"Not bad," the cat said. "Now we'll try some balance."

It sprang out of the window. Jai leaped, grasped the top of the window, and swung his legs out easily, landing on his feet on the other side. He felt extraordinarily pleased with himself.

The cat was walking neatly along the parapet, a darker

silhouette against the dark sky, its white chest and socks glimmering in the faint moonlight. Normally nothing could have persuaded Jai to get onto that parapet. But practicing on the window had given him confidence. He stepped onto it with barely a moment's hesitation.

It was all right as long as he kept looking at the flat roof side on his right. But the other side fell away, at first sloping over the mansard, and then sheer to the ground.

"Breathe," the cat said. "Don't go tense. Breathe down into your feet. Let the stone hold you. Look ahead. Don't look down. And feel where your nose is."

Jai walked from the urn to the eagle and back again. High above the world he walked, almost as if he were flying.

The moon disappeared. Thick clouds were rolling in from the south.

Jai hesitated. "I can't see anything," he complained, clutching the urn more firmly.

"Then walk in the dark," the cat commanded.

"No! I'll fall!"

"You've walked it twice," the cat said. "You should know where it is by now. It's no different. It's still in the same place. Your feet know. Trust them."

He took a deep breath and stepped out again. The cat was right. His feet did know where the parapet was. If he didn't let his thoughts mess them up with fear, he could walk without faltering from the urn to the eagle, from the eagle to the urn.

He'd done it several times and then rain came, sweeping across the park in chilly gusts.

The cat shook itself. It obviously hated getting wet. "That'll have to do for tonight," it said, and sneezed. "At least it's a start. Come on, I'll take you back to bed."

Together they ran to the window and leaped through it.

"Close the window," the cat said rapidly. But as Jai pulled it down the old sash cord snapped, and the window fell with a crash. The glass shattered, pieces tinkling onto the floor.

The sound reverberated around the narrow landing, and almost immediately a line of light appeared under Mrs. Frumbose's door. Jai could hear the sounds of someone getting out of bed and shuffling across the floor. As he followed the cat top speed down the stairs, he heard a key turn in a lock and a door open.

"Who's there?" Mrs. Frumbose called. "Who's out of bed at this time of night?"

"Hurry," gasped the cat. "Good-bye!" It disappeared down the passageway toward the back stairs.

Jai jumped into his bed and slid under the covers. His face and hair were wet. He pulled the covers right over his head and dried his face on the sheet. If this is a dream, he thought, it's a very real one! And if that was dream rain, it's very wet!

Someone came into the dormitory. Jai guessed it was Mrs. Frumbose, though it was too dark to see her and he wouldn't have recognized her, anyway, as she still hadn't put

UNDER THE CAT'S EYE ● 59

in an appearance downstairs. But he could smell her—a disgusting smell of stale alcohol, cigarettes, and vanilla essence. He lay without moving, hardly daring to breathe. Mrs. Frumbose passed through the center of the dormitory, holding up a lamp so the light shone onto every bed. Jai forced himself to breathe heavily as if in sleep. The light passed once more around the dorm. One of the children muttered a sentence from a nightmare.

After a few moments, when everything was quiet again and the smell had left the dormitory, Jai fell into a sudden dreamless sleep.

In the morning he tried to convince himself it had been a dream, but the knees of his pajamas were still very slightly damp, and Mrs. Frumbose made a huge fuss at breakfast about the broken window. Roughly was sent to fix it.

"Mrs. F must have been drinking again," Seal whispered to Hugo, trying to hide her giggles. They were both in a state of suppressed excitement. Hugo looked unnaturally neat and ordinary in his school uniform. At breakfast Mr. Drake's eyes rested on him for a long moment, as if the headmaster was taking note of the change. Mr. Drake looked weary with sunken eyes, as though he, too, had spent a restless night.

Apart from Jai, Seal, and Sunita there was one other girl still in her own clothes. She was wearing black stockings and a long silver sweater. Mr. Drake gave the three girls a tired glance and then looked at Hugo again.

Hugo tried to smile back naturally. It seemed a long while before breakfast came to an end. Jai spent the time studying Mrs. Frumbose. The matron was tall and stooped, with iron-gray hair pulled back tightly in a bun, and a yellowish wrinkled face. She had dark shadows under her eyes, and a thin, mean mouth. She wore a close-fitting black dress in a shiny material like beetles' wings, buttoned up to the neck with steel buttons. Every now and then she gave Seal and Jai a grudging look, as if she suspected the worst of them, while she ate her toast in little nibbling bites. Finally she finished, dabbed at her mouth with her table napkin, and rang the bell for the end of the meal.

The children stood and spoke the Nexhoath words. Hugo gave Seal a dig in the ribs and joined in very loudly. Then they were dismissed to make their beds and do the housework.

On the terrace later, going through the exercises with Miss Arkady, Jai looked up at the stone parapet above the mansard and thought, I walked up there! He remembered the grace and fluidity of the cat and how he had felt when he'd tried to imitate it. It couldn't have been more different from how he felt now going one-two-three, bend-two-three, stretch-two-three.

NINE

The day went by with its confusing jumble of lessons, stern teachers, regimented children, and frustrating sports. That would all have been bad enough for Jai, but he was also worried about what Seal and Hugo expected him to do, and quite unnerved by Kitty and Roughly, who seemed to be following him around all day. No matter what he was doing, one or the other of them was always there, turning up after each class, hanging around during recess and lunchtime, watching him with steady, devoted eyes.

During sports, Roughly worked in the paddock, cutting dead trees for firewood. He worked quickly and methodically, raising his shaggy head every now and then to watch Jai. In the still, winter afternoon the soft noise of the handsaw was almost the only sound. On the sports field the children played with their usual silent, grim intensity.

Hugo played well and walked off the field flushed and excited.

"Well done, Hugo," Mr. Porteous said. "It's good to have you on the team."

"Little does he know," Seal whispered to Hugo as she joined him. "When are you going to see Mr. Drake?"

"How about now?" Hugo's eyes were shining with excitement. "I think I could take on any number of cannibal drackles before tea! Where are you going to hide to be on guard?"

Seal shivered. "I can't believe you're really going to do this. What if it all goes wrong?"

"It won't," Hugo assured her. "And if it does, Roughly will help." He gestured toward the paddock with his head. Roughly had packed up his tools and was following a little way behind them, the basket of firewood on his shoulder.

"I don't want Roughly to help," Jai said suddenly.

"Why not?" Hugo demanded.

"There's something creepy about him. And Kitty, too. They never stop watching me. It's like they expect something from me, but I don't know what it is."

"You've got to help us, Jai," Seal pleaded. "You're part of us now. You know, it's that thing, I don't know what it's called, when you just have to do something, even if you're not sure why and you don't want to, because you're part of the other people doing it."

Hugo gave her a friendly punch on the shoulder. "You're not making much sense."

Seal shook herself. "We'll wait outside the door. Try and leave it open a little so we can hear. At the first sign of anything wrong, we'll come leaping in!"

As the other children went upstairs to change, it was not hard to slip through the door into the hall without being seen. Seal and Jai moved into the shadow behind the Dead Baby chest, and Hugo stepped boldly toward the study.

Jai looked at the crack in the chest, deep and dark as if it led into a bottomless world. His skin prickled. He glanced away from it to the portraits on the walls. Their shadowy faces were just as ominous.

Hugo knocked loudly on the door of the study. They heard Mr. Drake's voice say, "Come in."

The door opened, and a shaft of light fell into the darkened hall. For a moment it lit the face in the largest portrait. The eyes seemed to be looking straight at Jai. And they were just like Mr. Porteous's.

Jai's skin prickled even more.

Mr. Drake said loudly, "Oh, Hugo, good to see you, my boy. What can I do for you?"

Hugo said boldly, "I thought you could advise me about my future."

"I'd be delighted," Mr. Drake replied. "I'd noticed you in your uniform. I had a feeling it might be time for us to have a little chat. Come in and close the door, please."

Hugo waggled his fingers behind his back at Seal, and did not shut the door completely.

They heard Mr. Drake speak. "I'll just make sure it's quite shut. Because of the draft, you see."

The door closed, and the light disappeared.

Seal breathed in Jai's ear, "Oh no!" She stepped out of their hiding place and was about to run to the study door when the door behind them opened and someone walked into the hall.

Jai could smell her at once. It was Mrs. Frumbose. She was carrying a lamp, and in its light Seal was immediately visible.

"Celia Abbott, what do you think you are doing here? Eavesdropping outside the headmaster's study? You really are the most troublesome child we have ever had at Nexhoath. Come here at once."

While Jai stood frozen alongside the chest, Seal made a rush for the front door and began to struggle with the bolts. Mrs. Frumbose reached her in three swift steps and grabbed her from behind.

"Let me go," Seal gasped. "Let me go! I've got to help Hugo!" She lashed out, kicking frantically.

Mrs. Frumbose put down the lamp and grasped her more fiercely. Seal twisted around and sank her teeth into Mrs. Frumbose's hand.

"You wicked child," Mrs. Frumbose cried. "You will go to bed at once. I shall speak to Mr. Drake about you in the morning!"

"No, no," Seal sobbed. "You can't send me to bed. I've got to be with Hugo."

"I think that friendship must be stopped. It's unhealthy. You are not to speak to Hugo for the rest of the term. You will move from your dormitory into the sickroom. I shall keep an eye on you up there."

Securing Seal with one hand, Mrs. Frumbose picked up the lamp with the other. Holding it up she looked around the hall. "Is anyone else here?"

Of course she saw Jai at once. "Is that the new boy? What are you doing here? It's bad enough that you are so disobedient, Celia, but to be leading a new boy astray like this . . . words fail me, they really do."

The bell rang, and there was a thud of footsteps in the passageway beyond the hall as the children went into the dining room for tea.

"What's your name, boy?" Mrs. Frumbose said icily.

"Jai," he replied. "Jai Kala."

She sniffed as though she didn't like his name at all. "You may go to the dining room for tea, Jai. I will let you off this time. I know Celia is the main culprit. I am taking her upstairs now."

Seal began to scream.

Jai could hear her screaming and yelling as he hurried into the dining room. He noticed the teachers exchanging looks that seemed to say, *Celia Abbott, again! The most difficult child we've ever had at Nexhoath.*

He found a place next to Sunita, who was sitting with the girl in black stockings and silver sweater. They were giggling together and playing some finger game that he couldn't quite see. Sunita called the other girl Fern.

Mr. Corio came up quietly behind them and rapped Sunita's knuckles with his slide rule.

"No games during meals, Sunita Chatterji; you know the rules."

Sunita turned pink and looked up fiercely. She opened her mouth to say something, but then she shrugged her shoulders. "It's not worth fighting them," she muttered. "But I'm not going to let them get to me, like they did to Jamie. And when I'm home and they're all still here, who'll have the last laugh then?"

She whispered urgently in Fern's ear. Fern shook her head.

"Sunita!" Mr. Corio warned.

Jai sat, eating mechanically without tasting anything— which was just as well, as the bread was stale and the buns as hard as stones. They settled heavily in his stomach giving him indigestion. The tea was strong and stewed. He thought longingly of home and the delicious food his mother made. The evening stretched gloomily ahead with the prospect of homework, more tasteless food for supper, and then another lonely night.

He looked around for Kitty, remembering the muffins, but there was no sign of her. Roughly was sweeping leaves on the terrace outside. Every now and then he glanced through the window, keeping an eye on Jai.

Halfway through the meal Hugo walked in. He waved cheerfully at Jai and, after making his excuses to Mr. Corio, came and sat down beside him.

Jai studied him in surprise. After all Seal's fears and predictions, and her dramatic reaction to being dragged away by Mrs. Frumbose, he could hardly believe Hugo looked so normal. He didn't seem changed in any way at all. It was true he didn't say very much, but that could have been because he was eating bread and rock-buns as fast as he could.

Finally Jai asked him quietly, "Did anything happen to you?"

Hugo looked puzzled.

"When you went to see Mr. Drake," Jai prompted.

"Ohh!" Hugo took another rock-bun and stuffed it in his mouth. "You were right, Jai. There was nothing strange about Mr. Drake at all. We just had a little chat. He was awfully nice."

Jai felt a wave of relief sweep over him. "So it was just a game you were playing?"

"Well, we didn't know it was a game, but yes, I suppose it was." Hugo washed down the bun with a great gulp of tea. "You know, Seal and I must have been a bit crazy, making all that stuff up." He smiled at Jai, looking a little embarrassed. "Where is Seal?"

"Mrs. Frumbose caught us," Jai whispered. "Seal bit her."

Hugo drew his breath in sharply. "Oh no! She shouldn't have done that!"

"She's been sent to the sickroom. She's got to sleep there in the future, not in the dormitory."

"Well, you can't bite people and not get punished,"

Hugo said reasonably, and leaped to his feet as Mr. Corio rang the bell for the Nexhoath words. Afterward, he ran to join some of the other boys as they left the dining room. Sunita and Fern also left together. Jai walked out by himself.

Outside Roughly casually packed up his things and left the terrace.

TEN

Jai had gotten used to following Hugo and Seal around and now that they were no longer there he wasn't sure what to do with himself. He was really glad Hugo seemed unmarked by his encounter with Mr. Drake, and it occurred to him that the best thing would be to try to tell Seal, so she could stop being so upset.

There was still a little while left before Prep started, and most of the children were in the sitting room. He saw Mrs. Frumbose go in the direction of the kitchen. He climbed unobtrusively up the stairs to the dormitory and was about to tiptoe up the next flight to the servants' quarters when he heard voices from the main landing. He froze by the door. He could hear them clearly.

Kitty was saying quietly, "I've made a start. You should take over."

Roughly replied, "I don't want to scare him. He doesn't seem very confident. The years away have affected him more than we thought."

"There's so much to learn and so little time," Kitty said.

"Where is he now?"

"I'm just going to check."

Before Jai could hide, the door opened and Kitty stepped into the passage.

She was carrying a glass of milk and a piece of cake on a plate. "What are you doing here, Jai? Is everything all right?"

Jai hesitated. He didn't want to get into trouble. Then he remembered Kitty's devoted eyes and Roughly saying he could do anything he liked.

"I'm going to see Seal," he said with determination. "Mrs. Frumbose sent her to the sickroom."

"Courage and a kind heart," Kitty said enigmatically, and smiled. "I was looking for you," she went on in her yowly voice. "I thought you might be hungry. Take this. I'll let you know if Mrs. Frumbose comes up." She gave Jai one of her inscrutable looks.

Jai took the plate and the glass of milk. He sipped the milk, then thought he should save it for Seal. He went up the stairs.

It was getting dark, and he had no lamp. There were no lights under any of the doors. He knew which was Mrs. Frumbose's, but had no idea which of the others was the sickroom where Seal was imprisoned.

He tried the door next to Mrs. Frumbose's very carefully and stepped into the room. He guessed it was Kitty's, because one of her spotless white aprons lay neatly folded on the small iron bed, but apart from that the room was bare. Jai looked around, puzzled by its emptiness. There were no ornaments or pictures. He stealthily opened one of the drawers. It was empty. So was the wardrobe.

He went out closing the door as quietly as he could. When he opened the next door Seal was right before him, sitting on a bed, her feet swinging angrily. She jumped up when she saw him, her face lightening.

"Have you seen Hugo?"

"He's all right," Jai said, holding out the plate. "Do you want some cake?"

"You are clever, Jai! Where on earth did you get that from?"

"Kitty gave it to me."

Seal rolled her eyes upward. "Oh, thank you, Kitty." She took a huge mouthful of cake and ate hungrily for a few moments. When she'd swallowed and taken a gulp of milk, she demanded, "What happened? You're sure he's all right?"

"He's fine," Jai said. "Nothing happened. He said Mr. Drake was nice to him. He's gone off with Jamie and the others."

Seal put the plate down as if the cake had turned into ashes. "That means Mr. Drake's got him."

"No, it just means there was never anything to worry about. Hugo said it was all just a game."

"I've got to see him!" Seal picked up the cake again and took another huge bite. She washed it down with milk. "You've got to keep up your strength," she explained to Jai. "Here, you have the rest of it."

He couldn't resist. It was certainly much nicer than the rock-buns he'd eaten for tea.

Seal tiptoed to the door and opened it. She listened. The house was silent. She went out onto the landing and down the stairs.

Jai followed her automatically. They passed Kitty in the shadows, but she just nodded to them and smiled without saying anything. Seal found Hugo in a sitting room playing checkers with some of the other boys. Jai thought one of them might be Jamie, but he couldn't be sure. They all looked very alike.

Seal stopped in the doorway. "Hugo!" she called.

"You're summoned by the girlfriend," laughed the boy that might have been Jamie. He threw a handful of ivory fish tokens onto the table and scooped up the checkers to start the game again.

"Seeeliaah!" another boy crowed.

Hugo laughed with them, but got up good-naturedly and came over to Seal and Jai.

"What happened?" Seal whispered. "What did Mr. Drake say?"

Hugo shrugged, avoiding her gaze. "Nothing happened, really. We just had a chat about the subjects I'll do next year, what I want my career to be, which school I'll try out for— Mr. Drake reckons I might get a scholarship."

"A scholarship?" Seal repeated dully.

"Yeah, you know, when the school pays your fees for you."

"I know what it means," she said more angrily. "I just don't know why you're talking about it right now."

"It's what I talked to Mr. Drake about."

"You went to confront a drackle in his den and you talked about scholarships?"

"Seal," Hugo said patiently, still not looking directly at her, "Mr. Drake didn't do anything. He was quite nice, actually. It was just a talk about my future and about getting the most out of school. All that drackle stuff that we used to go on about—that was just a game."

"No!" Seal said.

"None of it's true."

There was a raucous burst of laughter. Hugo looked over his shoulder at the boys.

"Come and play, Hugo," one of them called.

"Yes, just a minute."

"Hugo!" Seal grabbed his arm. A wolf whistle came from the group, and more noisy laughter. Someone was making smacking kissing noises. Hugo laughed, too, his face going slightly pink.

"Change your clothes," Seal said urgently. "What about your red sweater? What about the Patagonian wool? And the secret herbs?" She pulled hard on the scratchy woolen sleeve of his black jersey, as if she would pull it off him.

"Seal!" Hugo looked more and more embarrassed. "Don't!"

The boys' laughter grew louder.

"Where's my ring?" Seal shouted desperately.

Hugo pulled his arm away from her. "Do you know what it was? It's a baby's teething ring! I'm not carrying that around anymore."

"Then give it back to me."

Hugo's face went a darker color. "I haven't got it. Mr. Drake took it."

"Mr. Drake's got my ring?"

"Seal, it's something for babies!"

"It was mine," Seal said in anguish.

Hugo looked increasingly uncomfortable. "You could go ask for it back."

"He's got you!" Seal backed away, her eyes full of horror. "Whatever he does to people, he's done it to you, too!"

"He doesn't do anything to people," Hugo said. "And he hasn't done anything to me." When Seal didn't reply, he said, "We can still be friends."

"We are friends," she said in a low voice. "Nothing can ever change that. We'll always be friends."

"Hugo," yelled the boys, "Come finish the match!"

He went back to them. Seal stared after him for a moment and then ran abruptly from the room.

Jai remained in the doorway, watching the boys, hoping they might ask him to join them. But no one took any notice of him.

Hugo picked up a handful of fish tokens and looked absentmindedly at the checkerboard. He was trying to remember something that had happened in Mr. Drake's room. A lot of things had happened that he couldn't remember very clearly, but there was one thing in particular that troubled him. He shouldn't have left Seal's ring in Mr. Drake's room. He hadn't meant to take it out of his pocket. He'd meant to give it back to her.

But Mr. Drake had looked at him with his ancient eyes and had said, in a calm, quiet voice, "Hugo, there's something stopping me helping you. Have you got something in your pocket?"

And Hugo had taken it out, just to show it.

Mr. Drake had held out his hand, and Hugo had found himself placing the ring in it. Hugo remembered the look on the headmaster's face—it had been amazed, incredulous, and then greedy. Mr. Drake had closed his hand over the ring, shut his eyes, and a shudder had run through him.

Hugo shuddered, too.

"A goose walked over my grave," he joked to the others. The memory faded. A few minutes later he was deep in the game of checkers and had completely forgotten what had upset him.

ELEVEN

As he got ready for bed that night, Jai thought about the boys playing games in the sitting room. He liked checkers and was good at it. He wished he could play with them. He thought about some of the math puzzles he could show them. They would be surprised that he could work out so many in his head. He felt a surge of relief that none of Seal and Hugo's fears about Mr. Drake were true. He would put on his school uniform in the morning and start being a normal Nexhoath boy, just like his parents would have wanted.

He tried not to think of Roughly and Kitty and what he had overheard on the landing. They had nothing to do with him. He was not going to approach them for help.

As he brushed his teeth and washed his face, the thought came to him that perhaps Hugo should not have given Seal's ring to Mr. Drake. It made him worry about Seal. He hoped she wasn't crying herself to sleep in the sickroom. But surely Hugo would still be friends with her. Everything's going to be all right, he told himself firmly. Everything is perfectly normal. He was in bed before the disembodied voice came through the voice pipe warning of five minutes to lights-out, and was asleep in less than two seconds.

It seemed like only two seconds later that he awoke to find the cat on his feet.

He groaned and tried to hide under the covers again, but the cat was too quick for him, clawing the covers away. "Get up," it ordered, its voice even more insistent and bossy than before.

They went out through the window and onto the roof again. The moon was a little larger, and the wind had dropped. It was cold enough for Jai to see his breath in the air. The gray slates, the lead in the roof, and the huge skylight glimmered in the moonlight. He looked out over the park. It was like looking at a lake. Trees, statues, fences, rocks, all had a dense black reflection, cast by the moon. The three horses grazed heads down in the paddock. In the stillness he could hear the pull of their teeth on the grass.

"It's beautiful," said the cat behind him. "Not as beautiful as the other one, of course. But it'll do for now, for you to learn the lay of the land. We'll start with the house."

Jai started to protest. "I don't want to learn anything. I don't have to learn at night. I want to go back to bed."

"You must learn," the cat said crossly.

"Why?" Jai pleaded. "Why me?"

"Don't you remember anything?"

"What am I supposed to remember?"

The cat stared at him for a few seconds, saying nothing. Then its amber eyes gleamed, catching the moonlight as it shook its head from side to side.

"Never mind," it said. "It'll all come back in time. Come on."

Jai followed it as it crossed the roof. It leaped nimbly onto the furthest chimney and disappeared into it.

"I'm not doing that!" Jai exclaimed. He turned and ran for the window. In an instant the cat had streaked out of the chimney and cut off his escape. It arched its back, showed its claws, and hissed alarmingly.

"This is not a game," it spat. "You must start learning before it's too late. Now follow me."

Jai reluctantly followed the cat down the chimney. It was dark and smoky, and he was sure he could feel soot coming off all over him. But the chimney was wider than he'd expected, and there were little footholds almost like steps. The memory of his agility on the roof came back to him. He imitated what he could see of the cat's movements and became almost catlike himself, moving with stealth and accuracy.

The cat led him through a maze of secret passages, up and down chimneys, under floorboards, behind the wainscoting. One passage led from the chimney nearest the skylight down a tiny flight of stone stairs. Little peepholes let a faint light through from the hall, and Jai realized they were behind the portraits.

He could look through the eyes of the old-fashioned people in the pictures. He looked across the hall at the huge shadowy portrait. The moonlight fell on Mr. Porteous's eyes, giving them a desperate, pleading stare. A flickering shadow made the portrait's hands move as if they were reaching out to him.

He was glad when the cat urged him on. It made him take the lead until he knew the house from the inside out. They saw nobody else, and heard little—just occasionally, as they passed under a dormitory floor, the breathing of sleeping children, and once a dog barking on the other side of the wall.

They finally came up through a trapdoor in the floor of the barn. Jai realized it was no longer so dark. The barn doors were open, and in the graying light he could see the cat clearly in front of him. It was looking at him with a faint air of disappointment.

"You didn't feel anything unusual that time?"

"You don't call crawling around in the dark under the floorboards unusual?" Jai retorted.

"No sort of furry, swirly sensation?"

"No! Just cold and tired!"

The cat seemed to sigh. "You've got a long way to go. If only we had more time."

"More time for what?"

The cat looked as if it were thinking deeply about how to respond, but before it could answer they heard the noise of a car. The cat froze for a moment, then slipped behind a bale of hay. Jai crept to the side of the barn door and looked out.

An enormous, black, very important-looking car drove

slowly into the yard. The driver wore a uniform and a chauffeur's cap. The rear windows were tinted so Jai couldn't see if anyone was inside.

There was a creak from the direction of the house. The back door opened, and a small figure stepped out. Jai recognized the white fur earmuffs and gloves, though a dusky pink coat now covered the purple sweater.

"Sunita!" he whispered.

She heard him and waved. "Hello," she said loudly. "Well, that is, hello and good-bye! I'm going home. I don't like this place, so I wrote to Mommy and Daddy, and they sent the car for me."

She ran toward it. The chauffeur got out and opened one of the rear doors for her, a broad grin on his face.

"Hello, Canvey," Sunita said, trying to sound calm and regal, but not succeeding. Then she squealed, "I'm so glad to see you!"

"Me, too, Suni," he said. "We've missed you. The place has been so quiet without you."

Sunita jumped up and down, partly to keep warm, partly with delight.

Jai couldn't stop staring at her. "Sunita," he began.

"What?"

"Do you think Mr. Drake does something to people? Is that why you're leaving?"

"I don't know if it's Mr. Drake," Sunita said. "But the teachers used to be sensible and now they are idiots. And everyone is ending up the same and I don't want to be like that. Jamie used to be fun, and he changed. There's no one else here I like particularly. Well, Fern's all right, but she lets everyone push her around. So I'm leaving before it happens to me."

When Jai didn't say anything, she went on impatiently. "You could leave, too, you know. Everyone could leave. I don't understand why they all stay here. I told Fern to come with me, but she wouldn't. But you could. You're here. All you have to do is get in the car and leave now with me."

"I don't have anywhere else to go."

"What happened to your parents?"

"They've got to go back to India," Jai said miserably. "They're leaving at the end of the week. I have to stay here until they come back. When they've sorted out the visas."

"Oh, visas," Sunita said scornfully. "Daddy knows all about visas." She took a little gold-covered notebook and pen out of her shoulder bag and walked back toward Jai. "Write your name down," she commanded, "and your parents' names and address. Daddy can sort it all out. He's practically at the top of the Bureaucracy."

Jai wrote in the little notebook with fingers that were so cold, he could hardly hold the pen. Sunita danced from foot to foot while she waited.

"What are you doing out here, anyway?" she said. "And why are you in your pajamas? Were you walking in your sleep?" She stopped dancing and peered at him more closely. "You're all dirty! What *have* you been doing?"

Jai had no idea what to say in reply. He handed the note-book and pen back to Sunita. She put them in her bag and closed it with a snap. "You don't want to change your mind? You can stay with me until Daddy's sorted out your parents and their visas."

Jai thought there was nothing he would like more, but for reasons that weren't quite clear to him, it didn't seem possible. He shook his head. Sunita shrugged. "Good-bye," she said. "Just don't do anything anyone tells you to do, and you'll be all right. That's what I've always found."

"Would you wear the school uniform?"

"Never!"

Canvey helped her into the car, tucked a rug round her knees, and closed the door. She gave Jai a small wave.

He waved back as the car reversed, hissing and steam-ing, out of the yard. He felt terribly alone when it had gone.

The cat came out from behind the hay bales. It said nothing about Sunita and her surprising departure.

"Get a move on and get back to bed before anyone sees you," it said fiercely.

It was all very well for Sunita to talk, Jai thought. She'd obviously never been bossed around by a cat.

TWELVE

Jai fell asleep immediately only to be woken by the bell about an hour later. He could still hear Sunita's words ringing in his head. He wasn't sure if he had dreamed them or not, but when he looked in the mirror, he realized his face and pajamas were still sooty. He scrubbed off most of the soot with cold water and got dressed once more in his own clothes.

At breakfast there was no sign of Sunita. He hadn't been dreaming. She had definitely left. No one said anything about her. Jai envied her riding off in state in the grand car. He wished he could have ridden away that morning and were not at Nexhoath now. He wondered why he hadn't gone. Something had prevented him, some tie with Nexhoath and the people in it, so that he had been unable to leave. He didn't understand the feeling, but he didn't like it.

Seal's eyes were red and her face pale, as though she had been crying all night. Hugo was cheerful, but quieter than usual. He looked the same as his old self, and yet not quite the same. He had become more like all the other boys, and he blended in with them.

Seal watched him most of the day, but he did not speak to her or look at her.

The only other person still wearing home clothes was the pale, dark-haired girl called Fern. No one spoke to her, and without Sunita she looked lonely and lost. Jai wondered if he looked like that to all the other children. He suspected he did. It would be better to join in, be like Hugo and the rest of them, than to look as lonely and lost as Fern and Seal did, each in her own way.

Tomorrow, Jai thought. *Tomorrow I'm going to wear the school uniform, too.*

At teatime Mrs. Frumbose rang the little handbell that stood next to her plate and spoke into the silence.

"Fern Anspach?"

Fern stood up, paler than ever.

"Yes, Mrs. Frumbose?"

"Mr. Drake wants to see you in his study after tea."

"Yes, Mrs. Frumbose," Fern mumbled, and sat down. No one said anything. Mrs. Frumbose surveyed the room with her icy stare. Then she slowly got to her feet. Everyone stood and mechanically repeated the Nexhoath words.

"We are proud to belong to Nexhoath," the children chanted. "Glad to respect and obey our teachers, and thankful for our food."

Jai thought he would go to the sitting room after tea in the half hour before Prep, and maybe play some games with

Hugo, Jamie, and the other boys. But as he was going up the staircase Seal came after him, took him firmly by the arm, and guided him through the little door onto the main landing.

"What are you doing?" he hissed. "You'll get into even more trouble."

"I'm going to watch again," she replied. "This time you look out for Mrs. Frumbose. I've got to find out exactly what it is that Mr. Drake does. Then maybe I can get Hugo back."

She shoved Jai onto his knees, and they peered through the railings. Fern appeared below them, and they watched her knock on the door of Mr. Drake's study. The door opened. They heard him speak, saying something about Fern's future in a jovial tone.

"That's what he always talks about," Seal muttered. "What does it mean? What does he do?" Then the door closed, and they couldn't hear anything.

"Damn!" Seal said. "Where can we go to hear more? Outside the door?"

"Let's go," Jai begged her. "We shouldn't be here."

"Or outside the window?" Seal went on, taking no notice of him. "If we creep down the stairs, we can try the door and if that doesn't work we can open the front door and go outside to try at the window."

She began to tiptoe down the huge staircase. Jai looked round helplessly. The huge portrait hung on the wall opposite him, its eyes level with his face. They seemed to be staring straight at him. The eyes did look just like Mr. Porteous's. But the face kept changing in the half light. Now he could see Mr. Corio, now Mrs. Antrobus—and weren't those long, flexible hands Miss Arkady's? Then he saw a flash of Hugo in the mouth, not smiling like Hugo, but open in a silent plea.

Seal looked back and saw Jai wasn't following. She beckoned silently.

"I'll keep watch here," he mouthed back at her.

She shrugged her shoulders and made a face at him. He watched her bend down outside the door to Mr. Drake's study. She frowned, straightened up, then strode to the front door. She waved briefly to Jai, seemed to take a deep breath, and undid the bolts.

Jai froze as the door creaked open. He was sure Mr. Drake would hear it. The thump of his heartbeat in his ears made him feel sick and dizzy. He felt the draft as the cold air swept into the hall and up the stairs. Seal slipped out of the house and into the night.

There was a moment of complete silence and then a noise that made Jai's hair stand on end. A sort of scuttling and rustling, and a strange sound, almost like a baby crying. His skin crawled. He remembered the Dead Baby. Surely, surely the story couldn't be true! But the noise was coming from the chest.

He tried to cry out to Seal, but his voice stuck in his throat and he could say nothing.

The lid of the chest moved slightly as if something were trying to lift it. Then something started to emerge from the huge crack in the lid. Little hands, baby's hands . . . Jai gave a small scream. He shoved his fist in his mouth. No, they weren't hands, they were paws, the white paws of some small animal, which was trapped in the chest, yowling quietly.

He knew he should go help it, but he couldn't move. He watched, paralyzed with fear, as the animal struggled for a few moments. Then he realized the paws were hands after all. It was a person in the chest. The lid flew open, and Kitty stepped out.

Jai shrank back into the shadows on the landing.

Kitty turned and looked upward.

Despite the dim light she saw him at once. She put her finger to her lips, shaking her head at him. Noiselessly she closed the lid of the chest, then approached the front door, which stood ajar. Through his terror Jai remembered Seal. He tiptoed down the stairs, trying not to look at the portrait. "Don't close it, don't close it," he whispered. "Seal's outside."

Kitty made a small annoyed sound, slipped out into the darkness, and returned in a couple of seconds holding Seal by the arm.

Seal was struggling a little, but Kitty hissed at her. "Be quiet, be quiet. Mr. Drake mustn't know we're here."

Seal relaxed, as if she trusted Kitty. Both children followed her silently as she hurried down the passage and into the kitchen.

Roughly was seated at the table, anxiously digging at the wood with his nails. He leaped to his feet. "What's happened?" he demanded.

"Sit," Kitty replied. "Just act normal." She pushed the two children down onto the bentwood chairs and filled the kettle with water at the old stone sink. She placed it on top of the range, and began to get out milk and cups. She placed a plate of cookies on the table. Her whole demeanor changed. It was as if she were engaged in a perfectly normal everyday task.

Seal and Jai looked at each other, then at Roughly. No one said anything.

"You should have been at Prep," Kitty said loudly as the door opened and Mr. Drake stepped into the kitchen. "Why weren't you there?"

Seal and Jai both thought it was wisest to say nothing. They stared at the pine table.

"The boy must have gotten lost," Roughly said. "I was just showing him the way back to the classroom when he said he was hungry." He stared blandly at Mr. Drake and rose slowly to his feet. "Did you want something, sir?"

"I thought I heard noises outside my study," Mr. Drake said. His voice was strong, and his face unlined. He looked around the kitchen with an air of youthful excitement. "How cozy! But surely these children should be at Prep now?"

"That's what I was just saying to them," Kitty replied. "But the new boy was hungry, and I thought some tea would help him settle. Shall I make you a cup, Mr. Drake?"

"I am a little peckish," Mr. Drake replied, smiling smugly to himself. "You may bring it to me on a tray, in my study, in ten minutes." He gave them all the same smug smile and left the room.

"What happened?" Roughly started to say again, but Kitty held up a hand to silence him.

"One more cookie, Jai, then you must go to Prep."

The door swung open again. Mr. Drake stood in the doorway. "The noises outside the study?" he queried.

"I was cleaning the chest," Kitty replied. "You said it needed dusting."

Mr. Drake frowned. "In the future, clean in the mornings," he said. "Shouldn't you be cooking at this time of day?"

"Just about to start," Kitty said. "Sausage and mashed potatoes. Roughly's got to bring in the potatoes from the cellar and peel them."

"Then Roughly had better get a move on," Mr. Drake said acidly. Addressing no one in particular, he continued, "Servants really are impossible these days."

As he left, Jai was sure he heard a low growl.

Kitty started putting things on a tray with quick anxious movements. "Blast the man," she said. "As if I'm not busy enough already—and what's the matter with you?" she asked Seal suddenly.

Jai looked at Seal. She had gone pale and was gripping the table with whitened knuckles as if she were going to fall off her chair. She didn't reply to Kitty or look up, but a tear fell from her downcast eyes and plopped onto the table's surface. She put a finger in it and wiped it away without saying anything.

"Speak up, girl," Kitty said. "What's the matter? Cat got your tongue?"

Roughly made a sort of growling cough. "Don't bother with her," he said to Kitty. "She's not our concern and we're not hers."

"Maybe we're all mixed up in this together," Kitty said as she went to the cupboard to get the teapot. "Sometimes you can't choose what's your concern and what isn't. Sometimes things just attach themselves to you and you've got to deal with them. That's the oddity. You should know that, Roughly, if anyone does. That's part of your nature after all." She poured a little hot water from the kettle into the teapot and rested it on the countertop to warm. Then she stood behind Seal and touched the girl lightly on the head. It was almost a caress.

"What were you doing outside?" she said quietly.

"I want to tell you," Seal replied in a muffled voice. "But I'm afraid you'll tell Mrs. Frumbose and I'll get into more trouble."

"I'd never tell that old fool anything," Kitty spit out. "Anyway, she's tucked up in bed with her headache mixture. She won't be down again tonight. Come on, you can tell Kitty, I won't give you away."

Seal didn't answer immediately. She leaned back in the chair against Kitty's white apron and twirled her hair next to her cheek. Kitty stroked her head more firmly.

"Didn't anyone ever hug you in your life, girl?" she said. "You're like a stray kitten, starved of affection. You shouldn't let people see you're so hungry for love. They'll take advantage of you."

"Kitty," Roughly growled, "don't get fond of her. She's not a kitten, and you can't just adopt her." He said sternly to Seal, "Why don't you go back to the classroom? And stay out of things that don't concern you."

Seal took no notice of him. She twisted around in the chair to look in Kitty's face. "I was outside trying to see what Mr. Drake does," she said. "I thought if I knew what he does I might be able to rescue Hugo."

Kitty's amber eyes met Roughly's dark ones. Kitty sighed. Roughly shrugged.

"Why do you work here?" Seal asked. "Where did you come from? And why are you so interested in Jai?"

Kitty said nothing for a moment. Then she said gently, "These are things that don't concern you. It's better and safer for you not to know."

"What about Jai?" Seal persisted. "Are you going to tell him these things?"

Roughly and Kitty looked at each other. They didn't say anything, but there was no doubt in Jai's mind that they were going to tell him. Sooner or later they would tell him why they were so interested in him, and what they told him would change his life forever.

"You hate Mr. Drake, don't you, Roughly?" Seal said.

"Will you help me get Hugo back from him?"

"It's not that simple," Roughly began. Kitty shot a warning look at him.

"Suppose I should keep my trap shut," he muttered.

"Why?" Seal demanded. "Why?"

The kettle changed its tune, and steam began to hiss from its spout. Kitty went to make the tea. She poured them each a mug, then left the room with Mr. Drake's tray. Jai and Seal stared at Roughly over the tops of their mugs. He didn't look at them. He was frowning, lost in thought, doggedly working something out. His lips started to move as if he were practicing a speech under his breath.

Suddenly what Jai wanted more than anything else was to get away. Things were happening without him knowing why, yet he suspected they concerned him deeply. He knew Roughly was about to speak to him, and once he'd heard what the man had to say there would be no going back. . . .

Going back? Going back from what? Jai didn't know and he didn't want to know.

Roughly lifted his head, looked straight at Jai, and opened his mouth, but before he could speak Jai leaped to his feet, pushing the mug of tea away so violently that it slopped over the table.

"Must go to Prep," he blurted out. "Come on, Seal." He pulled her to the door.

Roughly got to his feet, too. "Wait," he was saying. "Please . . ."

Jai turned. "Sit down," he said, more forcefully than he'd ever spoken to anyone in his life. "Sit down and stay there!"

He saw Roughly sink back into his chair, a beseeching look in his eyes, then he slammed through the door, nearly knocking Kitty over as she returned.

"Jai," she called after him in her yowly voice, but he didn't answer. He didn't want to hear what either of them had to say.

"Why don't you want them to help us?" Seal said as they went through the dining room and up the stairs to the classroom.

"They're creepy," Jai replied briefly. "If you ask me, they're even more creepy than Mr. Drake."

"You wouldn't say that if you'd seen what I saw in his study," Seal muttered.

"What did you see?"

They were nearly at the classroom. Seal looked around nervously as if they could be overheard. "I can't tell you here. We'll go to the Clumps tomorrow afternoon. Promise you'll come. I'll tell you everything there. And then you'll want help from anyone, even Kitty and Roughly."

THIRTEEN

Mr. Corio told off Jai and Seal for being late and made them sit apart. Halfway through Prep, Fern came into the classroom, her face expressionless. She was not wearing her black and silver clothes anymore. She had changed into the school uniform. She looked totally ordinary.

Jai looked across the room at Seal.

Seal was staring at Fern. She seemed about to speak, but Mr. Corio said to her sharply, "I've got my eye on you, Celia. Don't think I haven't. And I'm going to be watching you very carefully for the rest of this term. It's time somebody pulled you into line." Then he said cruelly, to the rest of the class, "Even her family didn't want this girl. Not surprising, is it?"

Seal dropped her eyes, and a red flush began to spread over the back of her neck.

No one looked at her. Everyone, including Hugo, carried on working industriously. Jai felt Mr. Corio's eyes on him, too. He prayed that the teacher wouldn't say anything sarcastic to him. He looked down at his gray-and-white shirt; he was glad he was wearing it. It reminded him of home and of his mother. But did it make him stand out too much? If he was dressed like everyone else would the teachers be less likely to notice him and pick on him? And would Kitty and Roughly leave him alone?

Thinking of Kitty brought the scene in the hall back to him. He began to tremble a little, remembering how scared he'd been. He'd thought it was the Dead Baby—that would have been bad enough, but somehow what he had seen was even worse. He kept picturing it over and over in his head: the little cat paws, the little hands, Kitty stepping out of the chest, her eyes when she saw Jai.

Seal didn't cry about what Mr. Corio said. Instead, she seemed to have become steely and cold inside. She didn't talk to anyone after Prep or during supper, but when they went upstairs to bed she dashed into the dormitory and collared Hugo on his own. "I've got to talk to you," she whispered. "Let's go to the Clumps tomorrow. Can you cut sports?"

"I can't," he replied. "I want to be on the soccer team. I've got training."

"I watched Mr. Drake through the window. I saw what he did to Fern. I need to talk about what happened to you."

"Nothing happened to me!" Hugo said loudly.

"Lights-out in five minutes," moaned the voice pipe.

"Come on," Hugo said reasonably, "we've got to get ready for bed."

"You don't believe me, do you?" Seal said, getting more

and more distressed. "You've forgotten all the things you used to say about Mr. Drake being a drackle. Just come to the Clumps. You'll remember there."

"All that was just a game!" Hugo exclaimed. "And I'm not playing it anymore."

Seal grabbed his arm. "I'm not going to let them keep you. I'm going to save you."

"I don't want to be saved," Hugo replied coolly and firmly. "And no one's doing anything to me."

As he tried to pull away from her, Mrs. Frumbose stepped a little unsteadily into the room.

"What's all this noise?" she said.

"Celia won't leave me alone, Mrs. Frumbose," Hugo explained.

Seal let go of his arm abruptly, staring at him with furious eyes, teeth gritted.

"Celia, you look as wild as an animal," Mrs. Frumbose said. "And you are not allowed in this dormitory. Go upstairs and go to bed at once."

Seal went to the door. She turned and spoke loudly into the silent dormitory. "That's the final proof, Hugo. If no one had done anything to you, you would never, ever have called me Celia."

Mrs. Frumbose pulled her out of the room.

No one in the dormitory said anything. They all went quietly to bed. Jai lay under the covers planning what he was going to say if the cat came in the night. He was going to tell it to go away, in the same way he'd told Roughly to sit and stay. He was not going to have anything to do with either of them.

Just before he fell asleep he remembered Seal's words to Hugo. It did seem strange that he would suddenly call her Celia. Hugo had changed, there was no doubt about that. Maybe he should go to the Clumps tomorrow to hear what Seal had seen in Mr. Drake's study.

The cat did not come. It was on the bed in the sickroom, keeping a very unhappy Seal company.

"No one is allowed to speak to Celia Abbott," Mr. Porteous announced at breakfast. "She has been a very naughty girl, and her punishment is that everyone shall ignore her until further notice."

Everyone turned and looked at Seal, who sat with downcast eyes, staring at her plate. Jai felt terribly sorry for her. And he thought Mr. Porteous was being very unfair. He remembered all the times he had been made to feel different at Sherbrooke—nothing as cruel as the way Seal was treated, but little things, boys mimicking his accent, making fun of the food he took for lunch, asking stupid questions about his mother's saris and why his father didn't wear a turban. At Nexhoath everyone was forced to be the same, but maybe it would be better just to allow everyone to be different, and enjoy the differences? He looked around at the silent, serious children. He missed Sunita and her purple sweater, and

Hugo's red one, and he missed the way they used to be, the *difference* they brought to the classroom.

Seal sat at her desk, proud and silent, throughout the morning. At lunch she ate on her own. Jai felt more and more sorry for her, and even more outraged at the way she was being treated. At rest time she was sent back upstairs to the sickroom.

Jai went to the dormitory and got out one of his books of math problems. But he couldn't concentrate on them. He kept thinking of Seal, alone and friendless upstairs.

So after rest time he didn't follow the other children out to the sports field. Instead he tiptoed up the staircase toward the servants' quarters and the sickroom.

To his surprise Seal was on the top landing, shoes in hand. She put a finger to her lips and gestured at Mrs. Frumbose's door.

"I'm not meant to be going out," she whispered to Jai. "But Mrs. Frumbose has fallen asleep, so I thought I'd creep away."

As she spoke, a creak came from Mrs. Frumbose's room. They heard a loud cough, then the sound of someone getting out of bed.

There was only one way to go. Jai grabbed Seal's hand. "Come on," he whispered, and hurried her toward the window.

Roughly had fixed it well. It slid up easily. Jai swung himself out and held out a hand to help Seal.

On the roof she stared at him in amazement. "Where are we going?" she asked, quickly putting on her shoes.

"I know a secret way out of here," he replied quietly. "Just follow me."

He led her across the roof and down one of the chimneys he had explored with the cat. It was large enough for them both to fit in comfortably, but it was rather sooty, and when the chimney branched they had to follow the smaller path, which was a tight fit. Their faces were smeared and blackened when they emerged from the fireplace in what had once been the housekeeper's sitting room.

Seal started to smile when she saw Jai. "Do I look like that?" She rubbed her sooty hands over her face. "Great camouflage," she explained.

Jai was checking out the room. It had a little round window that opened onto the backyard, and there was a small door in the wall, which he knew was a cupboard. At the back of the cupboard was a narrow space that led behind the wainscoting of the house.

He pulled Seal into the cupboard and closed the door behind them.

"Down here," he said. "You have to wriggle through."

Eventually they came out in the pantry. In the pantry floor, half hidden by huge cans of tomato soup and strawberry jam, was an entrance to one of the cellars. From the cellar they crossed under the stable yard. It was as dark as night down there, and Seal hesitated, but Jai adjusted his eyes almost unconsciously until he could see quite clearly. He took her hand and led her through the passage, then they clambered up rough steps that led into the barn behind the stables. Now, as well as being sooty, they were itchy from old chaff and wheat dust. But the barn's rear doors gave out onto the meadows, and the barn itself hid them from the house.

They made their way without speaking up the hill, zigzagging along sheep tracks, hiding behind outcrops of rock and bushes that clung to the steep slope. The Clumps rose before them, dark but not unwelcoming in the pale afternoon sunshine. Once they were under the pines, they started to relax. The trees absorbed them like their own shadows. No one would see them here.

The smell of the pine needles was sweet and soothing as the children walked swiftly to the rocks. The magic of the place wound itself about them. Jai sat down, feeling calmer than he had for a while.

Seal sat next to him. She was panting. When she got her breath back, she said curiously, "How did you know that secret way? There really is something strange about you, Jai. Where *do* you come from?"

He was going to deny it, to say again that he was no one special and that he came from a very ordinary house and family in the city, but there was a kind of admiration in Seal's eyes that appealed to him, so he said the first thing that came into his head instead, the thing he had not been able to get out of his mind.

"Kitty is a cat," he said. "I saw her last night. She came out of the Dead Baby chest as a cat. And then she turned into a person, into Kitty. And I don't know what Roughly is, but I don't think he's a real person, either. Neither of them are. They come from somewhere else."

"Where you come from?"

"No!" he shouted loudly. But he couldn't deny the thought any longer. He looked at Seal with helpless eyes. "Maybe. But what if I do? What do they want from me? I don't understand any of it."

"Kitty's nice," Seal said slowly. Her eyes brightened. "The sweetest little cat came and slept on my bed last night. Was that Kitty? Oh, I love Kitty," she went on extravagantly. "I wouldn't be frightened of them if I were you. They don't want to hurt you. They like you. More than like. It's as if they worship you."

"What do they want me to do?" Jai asked. He looked around the hilltop. The sun was still quite high, so there was no sign of the Cat's Eye. The bones lay white and gleaming in the sparse, coarse grass. In the distance Nexhoath stood, beautiful but menacing. Jai remembered someone saying, *Not as beautiful as the other one . . .* Who had said that? Of course, it had been the cat. And the cat had been Kitty. The cat had come to teach him about the other Nexhoath. But where was it? And was he going to have to go there?

Seal had picked up a piece of bone and was rubbing it

between her fingers. "I wish I still had my ring," she said. "I can't bear the thought of Mr. Drake having it." She shivered.

"What did you see last night?" Jai asked. "What actually happened?"

"I'm not imagining it," Seal said, "I know I'm not. I really did see into his study. It wasn't a dream."

"Did you think it might have been?"

"Sort of. Because I didn't understand anything I saw," Seal said. "It wasn't like anything I'd ever seen before. It was like something out of a fairy tale, something magic."

"What did you see? Try to describe it." Jai wanted to hear some plain facts that he might understand.

"Fern was standing in the study. And Mr. Drake was behind his desk. There was a thing on the desk, like a suitcase, and he opened it and looked at the lid. He played it with his fingers, as if it were a piano, but I couldn't hear if it was making any noise or not. Then he picked something up and aimed it at Fern."

"A gun?" Jai had read about guns in books, but never had actually seen one.

"I don't think it was a gun. It was like a small black box, with a glass eye in it. He held it out toward her and he was smiling and smiling, and then he looked from her to the suitcase and back again several times and smiled some more." She looked at Jai with furious eyes. "He kept smiling, that was the worst part."

"What did Fern do?"

"She just stood there. Like a rabbit when it's trapped by a stoat, you know."

Jai didn't know. He wasn't even sure what a stoat was, but it didn't seem to be the time to find out.

"Then, after a few minutes, he put the thing with the eye down and played just one note on the suitcase thing. And a little black thing came out of the side of it, like a very thin book, or a card. He's got a whole stack of them. I could see them on the shelves. He wrote something on it and put it with the others."

"It sounds like a dream," Jai said firmly. "I don't understand a word of it."

"I don't think I could have made it up," Seal said. "It's just too peculiar. Anyway, then Kitty came and grabbed me. I nearly died of fright. But I've been thinking about it all day. He steals something from people, and he stores it in those card things and it gives him new energy."

Jai shifted uncomfortably. The sun had disappeared, and he was feeling cold and shivery.

"He does something to people," Seal said slowly, almost to herself, as if she were trying to work it all out. "And then they become the same. And they stay the same. Once they've been in to see him, they look like everyone else and they act like everyone else. They lose whatever it is that makes them different. They lose what's going to take them forward. They lose their future." She grabbed Jai by the arm and then looked at him directly. "He says he wants to talk to them about their future," she whispered. "And he always laughs about it as if it's some sort of joke. But what he does is, he steals their future; he stores it and that keeps him always young. And he's done it to all the teachers, and everybody in the school, except us."

Jai was shivering and shivering.

"So he really is a sort of drackle," Seal muttered. "I always said he was. Do you know, Hugo and I started out thinking it was just a game we were playing. And now it's turned out to be the truth."

She got to her feet and stepped across to one of the pine trees. She put her arms around the trunk and hugged it, laying her face against the bark and closing her eyes for a moment. When she opened them, they were distant, focused on the school below. Down on the playing fields a fierce soccer game was in progress. Occasionally the sound of Mr. Porteous's whistle came to them on the wind.

"What are we going to do, Jai? There's only you and me left."

"Maybe we should run away," Jai suggested. "Like Sunita."

"Did Sunita run away? She was all right, really, wasn't she?"

"We should have asked her to help us," Jai said.

"It's too late now. And I can't leave Hugo. I'm going to rescue him. At least, I'm going to have a shot at it."

They were both silent for a moment. The wind sighed overhead.

"And, anyway," Seal went on, "neither of us has got anywhere to run to." She looked around at the place beneath the trees. "I love it here. I always feel safe here. I wish I could run away to somewhere miles from Nexhoath where I'd feel safe all the time. But even if that place existed, I don't think I'd be happy there unless Hugo was safe, too."

"I just wish I could go home," Jai said quietly.

FOURTEEN

Mr. Porteous's whistle blew one last long blast. Sports were over for the day. From the Clumps, Seal and Jai could see the children marching back to the house in an orderly line.

A black-clad figure appeared on the terrace waving its arms and looking this way and that. Even from a distance it looked furious.

"Oh no," Seal groaned. "It's Mrs. Frumbose. She's found out I'm not there. What are we going to do, Jai? Do you think we should stay up here?"

"I'm freezing," Jai said. The lights were coming on in Nexhoath, and the big old house looked almost welcoming compared to the gathering twilight and the cold wind up on the Clumps. But apart from wanting to be inside, he had come to a decision. The only way to help Seal was to go to Kitty and Roughly, and face whatever it was they had to tell him.

"We'll go back to the school," he told Seal. "I'll show you the secret way in, and we'll go to the kitchen and find Kitty."

But as they moved out from beneath the shadow of the pine trees, they heard shouting in the distance.

"Get down!" Seal hissed.

They slid back into the shelter of the Clumps to watch what was happening below.

The orderly line of children had broken up into a jostling, yelling mob. They seemed to be surrounding something, taunting and teasing it.

The mob broke for a moment, and a dog dashed out. Some of the boys picked up stones and threw them at it. One of them had a stick and began to run after the dog, trying to hit it.

"Oh, the poor thing!" Seal cried.

The dog raced up the hill toward them, as if it were heading for the safety of the Clumps.

Mr. Porteous stalked out from behind the barn, holding something long and black in his hand. He raised it level with his head.

As the dog came closer Jai could see it was the sort of dog he was most afraid of—big, with a long jaw and a shaggy gray-and-black coat. It was nearly as tall as him, and its paws were huge with long black claws. Its eyes brightened when it spotted him. It was running toward him, its huge tail wagging, its lips drawn back over its teeth as it panted. The teeth were white and sharp and enormous.

Then there was a distant crack, and the dog stumbled. Seal screamed. Something red flowered on the dog's shoulder. It fell, struggled to its feet, ran onward on three legs. The crack echoed again.

"What is it? What is it?" Jai shouted to Seal.

"It's a gun. Mr. Porteous has a gun!"

Jai's stomach twisted in sudden sickness. The idea that Mr. Porteous, standing so far away, could hurt something so close to Jai appalled him. And if he could shoot a dog, what was to stop him shooting two rebel children?

"Here, boy, here, boy!" Seal was calling the dog quietly.

It limped to them. Its eyes were dark with pain, and blood flecked its coat, but there was something about its face that Jai recognized instantly.

"Roughly?" he whispered.

"You're here!" Roughly said in relief as they helped him into the shelter of the rocks. He began to lick the gunshot wound with his tongue. "We thought we'd lost you. I was looking for you and then I started to shift shape too soon. I was trying to get back to the chest, but Porteous came out with his gun." He flexed his shoulder and winced. "It's not bad, nothing's broken. But you'll have to help me. Get back to the house and tell Kitty what happened. You know the secret ways now, don't you?"

Jai nodded.

"I'll get back when the Cat's Eye rises. Tell her to have the door open. Tell her Drake is getting suspicious. We may have to leave earlier than planned."

There was something about the way he said "we" that made Jai's heart sink. Seal noticed it, too. "You're not going to leave me on my own at Nexhoath, are you?" she said.

"What we do doesn't concern you," the dog replied.

"So why should I help you?"

"I'm not asking you. I'm asking Jai."

"Well, I'd help you, anyway," Seal said, "because you're an animal. But I think you ought to do what you can to stop Mr. Drake and rescue Hugo."

Roughly lay down on the grass, his head on his paws. "Go find Kitty," he said to Jai. "Stay close to her until I get back."

When the children emerged from the rocks, the grounds of Nexhoath were deserted. There was no sign of Mr. Porteous or Mrs. Frumbose. Everyone had gone in for tea. Seal led the way down the hill, and they reached the barn without seeing or hearing anyone. Then Jai took the lead to guide them back to the kitchen.

But as they crept behind the bales of meadow hay, they heard footsteps outside the barn. Seal peeped round the side of the bales. "Mr. Porteous!" she mouthed at Jai and she pantomimed pulling a trigger with her fingers. Jai couldn't resist taking a quick look, too. Mr. Porteous was standing in the doorway of the barn, silhouetted against the fading evening light, the gun a long, black stick shape close to his side.

As Jai slid back behind the bales, they heard the teacher step farther into the barn. Jai pulled open the trapdoor to the passage below, his fingers slipping on the cold iron ring. Seal helped him frantically. They could hear themselves making an awful lot of noise. And they couldn't prevent the trapdoor from falling behind them with a thud.

Kitty's amber eyes widened with alarm when she opened the pantry door and saw Jai and Seal emerge from the trapdoor in the floor. They were covered with soot and dust, they were cold from their trip through the dark, damp passages, and they were starting to feel really frightened.

She sat them down by the range and pushed mugs of scalding tea into their hands. "Jai, tell me what's happened."

"Roughly is up at the Clumps," Jai said. "He's in his dog shape. He's been shot, but it's not serious. He'll come back when it's dark, when the Cat's Eye rises."

"You've got to leave the front door open for him," Seal added, taking a huge gulp of her tea. "And he said Mr. Drake is getting suspicious and that it's time for you to leave."

Jai spoke through chattering teeth, "Mr. Porteous had a gun! He must have heard us in the barn. He won't follow us here, will he?" He looked anxiously at the pantry door.

Kitty prowled this way and that, shaking her head. Jai thought that if she had a tail she would have been lashing it.

"You know what Mr. Drake does, don't you?" Seal asked.

"We know what he does," Kitty yowled. "But we don't know how he does it."

"Why don't you stop him?" Seal was almost crying. "We've got to do something about Hugo!"

"You don't understand," Kitty replied. "Mr. Drake is a terrible creature, an evil criminal, an exile from a world beyond this one. He uses something he brings from that world to enslave people, and we don't know how to stop him. All we can hope to do is keep him out of our world. To do that we have to close the gateway by taking Jai home. Roughly and I came for Jai." She looked toward Jai and smiled.

He shrank back in his chair. "What do you mean, came for me?"

"We came to take you home," she said gently. "You don't belong here. You belong in our world. We've been looking for you for years. You were lost a long time ago, but now we've found you and it's time for you to go home."

Jai had a sudden picture of his parents, back in the house in the city. That was his real home. If he wanted to go anywhere, it was there.

"No!" He shook his head stubbornly.

"Where will you take him?" Seal demanded. "And what does the chest have to do with it?"

"It's a door between the worlds," Kitty replied. "This isn't the only world, you know. This is known as the ninth world of Nexhoath. There are lots of worlds, all stacked up, and all slightly different. Different options, different directions, all branching out endlessly. If you can travel between the worlds you have a lot of power. Not many people can. And some are good, like Roughly and me, and some are bad, like Mr. Drake."

"Does Mr. Drake come from the same world as you?" Seal asked.

"Certainly not!" Kitty made her tail-lashing face again. "Ours is the eighth world. At first we thought *this* was Mr. Drake's world, but he has different powers from people here. He must come from somewhere else—maybe from the tenth world of Nexhoath. He may even have been exiled there from somewhere beyond. A lot of criminals are, you'd be surprised. The tenth world is comparatively easy to get to. It's like a way station. It collects a lot of riffraff."

"If I come from another world, what about my parents?" Jai voiced his most terrible thought. "Who are they? I know they're my real parents, I know they are."

"They looked after you for all those years," Kitty said. "We'll always be grateful to them." She took a quick look at Jai's face and went on. "You don't need to know everything all at once. We were going to tell you gradually, after we'd had time to teach you more. But time's running out . . . we can't run the risk of Mr. Drake getting his hands on you and we must close the gateway to keep him out of our world. While we've been looking for you Roughly and I have had to keep going back and forth. We can only keep this world's shape for a few hours at a time. Then we start to shift back again. That's what happened to Roughly. We have to pass through the chest to regain our power."

Kitty paused and looked out the window. It was nearly dark. She reached out and patted Jai on the arm.

"The Cat's Eye will be rising. Roughly will be here soon." She took a deep breath, then continued in a steely voice. "I'm going to open the door and the chest. Jai, we're going to take you home. So you have to say good-bye to Seal."

"You can't leave me here on my own!" Seal's voice rose to a squeak. "And what about Hugo? You can't let Mr. Drake go on like this. What about all the other children?"

Kitty opened her mouth to answer. From outside the kitchen window came a short, urgent bark. Jai recognized it as the barking he'd heard several times before. Mr. Drake had been mistaken. There *had* been a dog at Nexhoath.

Kitty gave a small sigh of relief. "He's back safely. We must go now." She stood up and collected a feather duster from a hook on the wall. "I'll pretend to be cleaning. Come, Jai."

"Please don't leave me here," Seal wailed.

"Do you think I want to? Don't make it harder on me," Kitty yowled in frustration. "But I can't take you. Going through the gateway would change you. It might give you powers you don't want or need. You must stay in the world you belong in."

She pulled Jai to the door. Seal jumped up and went with them. "You won't get rid of me," she said. "I'm not letting you go until we've saved Hugo."

Before Kitty could open the door, it swung toward her.

Mrs. Frumbose stood on the threshold.

"Whatever is going on?" she inquired in her most icy voice. "Celia, did you disobey and leave the sickroom?"

"Looks like it, doesn't it?" Seal replied insolently. "How else would I have gotten down here?"

"Kitty, where are you taking these two children? I think they should be at Prep now."

"Jai's not doing Prep tonight," Kitty replied, pushing past Mrs. Frumbose and pulling Jai after her.

"Bring Seal, too," Jai said quietly.

"I can't!" Kitty hissed at him.

"Do it," he commanded. "I'm not going with you unless Seal comes, too."

"Excuse me," said Mrs. Frumbose. "No one is to go anywhere." She stepped closer and peered at the children. "What have you been doing? You are absolutely filthy!"

Seal tried to dart past her. Mrs. Frumbose seized her by the sleeve of her red sweater. Seal kicked her in the shin.

Mrs. Frumbose gave a kind of grunt, and at that moment Mr. Drake's voice came echoing grotesquely through the voice pipe.

"Jai Kala to my study immediately, please."

"I'll take him," Kitty said.

"Seal, too!" Jai ordered her.

"Oh, very well," Kitty gave in. Trying to look as if she was glaring fiercely at Seal, she added, "and I'll take this naughty child, too. Mr. Drake shall deal with her."

"Certainly!" said Mrs. Frumbose. "That will give me the greatest pleasure."

Kitty held each child firmly by the arm. As they went through the door into the hall she whispered to them, "Be ready to jump into the chest as soon as Roughly's in."

"Me, too?" Seal said.

"Yes, you, too. What happens, happens. Jai won't go without you."

The hall was silent and melancholy in the gathering darkness. The portraits on the walls gazed gloomily down onto the three small figures. Shadows lay in all the corners. The black crack in the lid of the old chest looked ominous.

Putting her finger to her lips, Kitty tiptoed across the polished floor and pulled back the bolts on the front door. It creaked as it swung open. Kitty gave a low whistle, and the big dog padded panting into the hall. Its eyes gleamed wild and green, there was blood on its muzzle, and it looked exhausted. Casting a grateful glance at Kitty, it bounded toward the chest.

Kitty held the lid open. Roughly leaped in.

The door of Mr. Drake's study opened. They heard Mr. Drake's voice say, "Is that you, Jai?"

Kitty grabbed Jai and pulled him toward the chest. As she pushed him into it, Mr. Drake stepped into the hall, holding up a lamp. The light fell on Seal.

"Celia!" Mr. Drake said. "You don't seem to be able to stay out of trouble, do you? I was expecting Jai, but never mind. I was going to call you to my room sooner or later. We may as well make it now. Come in, my dear. We'll talk about your future."

Seal made a grab at the lamp, knocking it from Mr. Drake's hands. It fell to the ground, the glass shattered, and the flame went out.

In the sudden darkness Kitty yowled, "Quick, Seal! Quick. Get in!"

Seal dived into the chest. Kitty jumped in after her and pulled down the lid.

FIFTEEN

For a few moments absolutely nothing happened. Then the lid of the chest flew open again, and Roughly and Kitty jumped out.

"Don't get out," Seal was crying. "Don't get out! He's there, he's there!"

"It's all right," Kitty meowed.

Jai climbed carefully out of the chest. He looked around with wide eyes. He was in the front hall of Nexhoath, but it was not the same as the hall he had just left with its frightening shadows and Mr. Drake's evil presence. Everything in it looked fresh and new. No gloomy portraits hung on the walls. Instead, the pictures were cheerful ones of animals and people together. Light poured through the hall from hundreds of candles. The chandelier sparkled. The rugs glowed with color. Everything seemed to emanate life.

Seal grabbed Jai's hand and pulled herself out of the chest. She tiptoed to the door of Mr. Drake's study and looked in. "He's gone," she said in amazement. "And all the strange things in there have gone, too, the cards and the suitcase thing." She sniffed the air. "It smells different here," she said. "Where's Mr. Drake?"

"Not in this world," Kitty said.

"Not yet," Roughly muttered. They were both in animal shape, but they looked slightly different from before, as though they were where they belonged. Their bodies were more fluid and relaxed. It was obvious, if you looked carefully, that they were back in their own world.

"I suppose we couldn't really leave the girl there with him," Roughly went on.

"Certainly not," Kitty said, purring around Seal's feet. "There's a risk to her, but it couldn't be more dangerous than being abandoned to Mr. Drake. And maybe it's the oddity. You can't fight the oddity."

Then she looked up at Jai. "Welcome," she said. "Welcome to your own land."

"Yes," Roughly added, his tail swinging from side to side. "Welcome, master."

Seal turned from the doorway and stared at the three of them. "There," she said to Jai. "We knew you were someone special. You *are* a prince, aren't you?"

"Am I?" Jai said to Kitty. The idea made him feel sick.

"This is your world," she said. "You are needed to hold it together and protect it. Is that what being a prince is?"

"I don't know," Jai said. "I don't know anything anymore."

"Believe us," Roughly said. "We've been searching for you for a long time. Let's get something to eat. Then we'll tell you everything. It's so good to be home and to have gotten you home safely." He barked joyously. Kitty was purring.

The doors from the kitchen swung open. A crowd, human and animal, came bursting into the hall. They exclaimed in delight when Kitty pointed to Jai. Dogs barked, cats purred, birds sang triumphantly. The women dropped curtsies. Men and boys patted Roughly on the head and shook him gently by the paw, exclaiming over his injured shoulder. One of the boys ran for water to bathe the wound. Then they shook Jai's hand, too, saying over and over again, "Welcome, welcome home!"

Jai shrank back a little. The hands seemed rough and clumsy to him. And the animals kept pressing up against him, wanting him to stroke them. He wasn't sure he liked their smell or the feel of their fur. If this was home, he wondered, did that mean he had to stay here forever?

After Jai and Seal had washed off the soot and the dirt, they went into the dining room for dinner. It was the same room as in the other Nexhoath, with the same terrace outside, and the same statues, only here the plants in the tubs were green and healthy. Everyone, humans and animals, sat on the floor together. The humans made sure the animals had enough to eat and cut up the food into neat pieces for them.

Many of the beings could shift shape. A hare at the end of the room shimmered into a beautiful girl and danced wildly with an owl, who then fluttered to the floor and became a young man. An older man sang a haunting song, accompanying himself on a harp, then shifted into wolf shape and howled the same tune.

Seal stayed close to Kitty, eating little but watching everything with fascinated delight. When the meal was over, most of the beings shifted into animal shapes, laughing and joking. Those who were left as humans had to go out to the kitchen to do the washing up. Kitty took Seal and Jai into the room that in the other Nexhoath was Mr. Drake's study.

A bright fire burned in the grate. Roughly, who had followed them from the dining room, stretched out in front of it, wincing slightly in pain.

"Don't sleep yet," Kitty said. "We must do a little explaining first."

Roughly yawned, showing his huge white teeth. "Can't it wait till morning? I'm worn out."

"Dogs," Kitty said, lashing her tail. "All they think about is eating and sleeping."

"Put another log on the fire, Jai," Roughly said.

"You're the servants," Seal said as if she were trying to work something out. "So why do you ask Jai to do things for you?"

"Who said we were servants?" Roughly replied sleepily, rolling over to warm his other side.

"In some ways we are like servants," Kitty said. Her eyes gleamed orange in the firelight. She looked wide awake.

Jai stood up and put a log carefully on the fire. He took

a poker from the hearth and gave the logs a prod. Sparks flew upward, and then flames started to lick at the wood.

Roughly gave a deep sigh of contentment. "Thanks," he muttered.

"And in other ways," Kitty went on, "Jai and the other humans are our servants."

Roughly waved his paws in the air. "We've got no hands," he explained. "People who have hands can do some things we can't do. And vice versa. For instance, you can't bark."

"I can bark," Seal replied, and proceeded to demonstrate. "Woof! Woof!"

"Would that scare you?" Roughly said scornfully to Kitty. "Would that keep strangers away?"

"Maybe not," Kitty admitted. "But we don't need to argue about that. The point is that here in this world people and animals live as equals. Animals can speak, unlike in your world, and no one makes them slaves. Here everything has a voice. Even the trees and the rocks speak to us."

"Like at the Clumps," Seal whispered, her eyes shining.

Kitty rubbed her head against Seal's hand. "Every being does what it does best," she went on. "Horses are fast, but they can't cook. Cows don't mind sharing milk, but they can't build houses or barns for shelter. People have hands, so they help by doing things that the other beings can't do for themselves."

"Rub them behind the ears, for example," Roughly said, pushing his great head toward Jai.

Jai reluctantly put his hand out and patted the dog. "Why did I end up in the other world?" he said slowly. "Why didn't I just stay here? It would have saved a lot of trouble."

"Now we have to try to explain it all to you," Kitty said.

Roughly seemed to be asleep, but his green eyes were half open, watching Jai's face as Kitty told her story.

"You know that we can travel between the worlds," she began. "In our world we have perfected the art of shape-shifting. All the species live very close together and understand each other, so we find it easy. And it's especially useful when traveling between the worlds. Some worlds, the ninth and tenth worlds of Nexhoath, for example, are like hell for animals, so anyone traveling there takes human shape for as long as possible. But we can't keep it without returning to our world to recharge, as it were, which is why Roughly turned dog again too soon.

"This house, Nexhoath, was built on a place of power, a pivot, where the worlds meet and branch off from each other. Its name comes from *Nexus,* which is a link, or a network, and an old word, *hoath,* which is a mixture of *heath* and *hearth: heath* for the animal world and *hearth* for the human world. This is where the animal world and the human world are linked. No one knew about the place of power, until the baby was hidden in the chest. . . ."

"So that story was true," Seal gasped.

Kitty nodded. "The baby was so young and new that it

didn't know the powers it had. It managed to escape, and in escaping it opened another world, in which it lived but without parents. In the world you come from the baby died, and Nexhoath became a place of negative forces."

"Which would explain why Mr. Drake could get to it and operate there," Roughly observed.

"Probably," Kitty agreed. "But there is never negative without positive. And so in our world, which started at that moment and at the same time had always existed, Nexhoath is a place of life and goodness. Its energy is all positive."

Jai's head was spinning. Seal screwed up her eyes as if she was trying to make sense out of what Kitty was saying.

"It's a paradox," Kitty said apologetically, and licked Seal's hand with her rough little tongue. "Hard to understand, but the only way to explain things that seem to contradict each other, but are actually the same. You have to grasp it as a whole. Trust me."

"Oh, I do trust you," Seal replied with feeling. "And I know you're right about Mr. Drake. He's the most evil person I've ever known. But where does Jai fit into all this?"

"In the new world, Nexhoath Eight, the baby was looked after by animals and grew up to be a strong and wise person. Since then, in every generation another baby is born who has the same powers and the same wisdom. And it's given two animal guardians to make sure it grows up safely."

"You and Roughly," Seal said.

"Well, it wasn't us to start with." Kitty sighed. "If it had been, none of this would have happened. It was two others. I'm afraid they weren't very responsible. It's an enormously important job. This child holds our world together, having human shape but being raised by animals. He or she keeps the balance between humans and animals and makes sure no one species becomes too powerful."

"A little while ago, the mice got totally out of hand," Roughly commented. "Jai's predecessor had to take strong measures."

"So it is Jai," Seal said quietly.

"Yes, it's Jai," Kitty replied. She couldn't help smiling a small, refined cat-smile.

Jai felt the bottom of his stomach sink again, just like when he'd first seen Nexhoath. Had he known then, in some way, that this was the destiny he was heading toward?

"What was he doing in our world then?" Seal asked, frowning deeply.

"It's still a mystery," Roughly said. "The baby was brought to Nexhoath, to be taught in secret. No one knew its identity apart from its guardians. Then it disappeared. And *they* disappeared. I suppose they were ashamed and guilty. It caused us no end of problems before we realized what had happened." Roughly's ears drooped, and he gave a low growl.

"Well, there's no point getting in a state about it now," Kitty said briskly. "What's done is done. And who knows, maybe it was the oddity."

"You keep saying that. What does it mean?" Seal asked.

"It's what we say when something unpredictable happens and then it works out for the best. The oddity is a sort of destiny you can't escape from, like things you know you've simply got to do or people with whom you know your life is bound up."

"So that's what that feeling's called," Seal exclaimed. "The oddity. What a useful word."

Kitty purred again. "It is. And it's a very useful thing, too. You can always trust the oddity. Anyway, the baby disappeared."

"We searched everywhere," Roughly said, his eyes darkening at the memory. "We finally came to the conclusion that in some way history had been repeated. The baby had been placed in the chest and had found its way into one of the other worlds. We've been looking for it for many years. Finally we came to the ninth world."

"And found Mr. Drake had taken over Nexhoath," Kitty added.

"That complicated things enormously," Roughly growled. "Mr. Drake had discovered what seemed to him to be a perfect situation to exploit. A boarding school where he could quickly assume power, using methods from his own world that no one else knew anything about."

"We hoped the lost child, who would be eleven or twelve by now, would be drawn back to Nexhoath on the day the Cat's Eye rises," Kitty said. "That's a day of great power in our world because our legends tell us it's the day the first baby was hidden in the chest and opened up the new world. And it was on that day that Jai arrived at the school."

"We couldn't let you fall into Mr. Drake's clutches," Roughly said. "So we had to bring you here before you were really ready." He looked at Jai's unconvinced face and continued gently, "That's why it all seems so strange to you. There's a lot to get used to. You should have had many more lessons, shape-shifting and all that, but there wasn't time."

"I don't understand why my parents never told me I wasn't their son," Jai said.

"Theirs is another story," Kitty said. "One we don't know. Maybe they found you and adopted you. Maybe they had had a baby, but it died, and they simply pretended you were that baby. The oddity again, I suppose. They needed a baby to be able to have a chance to stay in that country that you found yourself in. Something to do with the visas and the rules for living there, isn't that right?"

Jai said nothing. If Kitty was speaking the truth, the truth made him terribly sad.

"Hey," Roughly said, "cheer up. We're all here together now. None of us got taken over by Mr. Drake, and even though I did get shot, I'm still alive and kicking. Chuck another log on the fire."

Seal stood up to do it. She didn't sit down again. She looked at each of them in turn, opened her mouth to speak, then closed it tightly.

"What's up?" Kitty said.

"You all belong here," Seal replied slowly, "but I don't, do I?"

"You can stay here, though," Jai said swiftly. "Can't she?"

"It's all very well saying that," Seal went on. "But what about Mr. Drake? What about all the children trapped at the other Nexhoath? And Hugo? Someone's got to do something about that."

Roughly gave a huge sigh.

"I can't stay here," Seal declared. "I'll have to go back and help Hugo."

"Please don't go!" Jai wailed. Seal was the only familiar person in this alien world—a world that was going to be his home. He couldn't bear it if she left him.

"She should go back . . . ," Roughly began.

"We'll talk about it in the morning," Kitty said sharply. "Jai's had enough for one day. It's a lot to take in. Right now, we all need some sleep."

She leaped up and crossed the room to where Seal was standing. She purred loudly as she wove between Seal's legs. "Sleep here tonight," she said. "You can decide what to do in the morning."

Sixteen

When Jai woke he was lying in the big bed in the grand bedroom that Kitty had offered him when he first had arrived at Nexhoath.

The room was bright with winter sunshine. He felt suspended between the worlds, as if he could choose which Nexhoath he was in. Thinking like that made his head spin. He wondered how many more Nexhoaths there might be. He imagined them disappearing into eternity, like the reflections in two mirrors.

He wondered if he would ever get back to the one that was his home. The thought puzzled him. Kitty and Roughly had told him he belonged in Nexhoath Eight. So why didn't he feel more at home here?

He got out of bed and went to the window. Kneeling on the low window seat, he looked out over the park. He had to rub the condensation off the window before he could see anything. It was freezing.

The low-slanting morning sun lit up a sparkling world, breaking the mist into soft flowing shapes. Jai saw one gray shape that remained solid and real.

It was a horse, grazing in the paddock. He wondered if

there were three horses, like in the world he had come from. When the mist cleared he couldn't see any others, but he saw Seal walking across the dew-soaked grass, leaving black footprints behind her.

Seal was talking to the horse. It threw up its head and seemed to be talking back to her. Of course—in Roughly and Kitty's world, animals could talk. Seal would love that. He wished she could stay in this world with him. Then he thought of Hugo and all the other children trapped in Nexhoath Nine. Somebody had to go back to rescue them. Maybe he should go with Seal. But Kitty and Roughly probably wouldn't let him. And the thought of Mr. Drake made him shiver. How could Seal think of facing him?

Then he thought of his parents. He longed to see them. He wanted desperately to go back.

For a moment his eyes blurred. He rubbed them and blinked. When he looked again there were two horses. And they were galloping, galloping around the paddock, shaking their manes and tails, kicking out in play.

There was no sign of Seal. Jai shivered. Cold air seemed to flow from the windowpane. He stared out of the window for a long time, but Seal did not reappear. Finally the cold drove him back to bed, until Kitty scratched at the door, telling him to come down for breakfast.

When he went downstairs Seal was in the kitchen eating porridge and throwing pieces of toast to two dogs who were sitting next to her.

"Hello," she said when she saw Jai. "Do you know, I've never had porridge before? I've only read about it in books."

"Is it nice?" Jai had never had porridge, either.

"It's okay. But, you know, it's the idea of it!"

Her face was flushed with color, and her eyes were bright. She looked wonderful.

"I saw you talking to the horse," he said.

The most enormous smile spread across her face. "Isn't he fantastic?"

"Then where did you go to?" Jai asked curiously. "You disappeared."

Seal tossed another piece of toast into the air. The dog's jaws snapped. She didn't reply, but she couldn't stop grinning. She shook her head like a horse shaking its mane.

Kitty jumped onto the table, a strange look on her face. She looked from Seal to Jai and back again.

"I wish I could stay here," Seal said wistfully. "This is the best place I've ever been in my life. But I can't leave Hugo with Mr. Drake." She took a last mouthful of porridge, gave the bowl to the dogs to lick, and stood up.

"What are you going to do?" Jai said. "How can you possibly stop him? He's obviously got the most amazing powers."

"I just have to go," Seal said. "It's the oddity. Hugo is part of the oddity for me. There's nothing I can do about it. I've got to go back. If I stay any longer I'll never want to leave. So I must go now."

"I'll come with you," Jai said.

"No, you've got to stay here. You've got to hold this world together. This is where you belong." The smile left Seal's face abruptly. "But I belong there," she said, sounding slightly doubtful about it. "So I'm going back."

Kitty's eyes were growing bigger and bigger. "Go and get Roughly," she said urgently to the dogs. They jumped up at once and bounded out of the kitchen.

"Dear old Roughly," Seal said. "He didn't want me to come here, did he? He'll be glad I'm going. Say good-bye to him for me."

"Wait, wait," Kitty yowled. She tried to reach Seal from the table with her paw, overbalanced, and slipped to the floor.

"You mustn't try to stop me," Seal said. "I want to stay here more than anything else in the world. But I've got to rescue Hugo. Good-bye, Kitty; good-bye, Jai. I'll never forget you."

Her face contorted as if she were about to cry. She swung abruptly around and ran out of the kitchen. The door slammed shut behind her.

"Open the door, Jai, open the door!" Kitty yowled, pawing at it in frustration.

Roughly bounded through the back door. "Where's the girl?" he shouted at Kitty. "Where's Seal?"

"She's gone back to the chest. Roughly, we must stop her!"

Jai opened the kitchen door, and they all ran into the passage.

"Did you know she's a shape-shifter?" Roughly panted. "She was galloping with the horse in the paddock!"

"I guessed. Just now," Kitty yowled as they tore down the hall.

The chest stood silent, its lid closed. Seal had gone.

Roughly howled.

"We'll have to follow her," Kitty said. "We'll have to go back."

"What's going on?" Jai asked slowly.

"We made a mistake," Kitty said, bewildered. "Where's the ring?" she said to Jai. "Why were you holding the ring?"

"It was Seal's. I found it in the driveway." He paused as the realization flooded through him. He wasn't at all disappointed. He felt the most enormous relief. "You got the wrong person, didn't you?" he said. "It's not me after all. It's Seal!"

SEVENTEEN

"We have to follow her," Kitty said again. "We can take Jai back, too." She pushed her nose against the back of his knee. "Sorry we involved you in all this."

"I don't mind," Jai replied. "I expect it was the oddity. But I'm awfully glad I can go back."

He held the lid of the chest open for Kitty and Roughly, then climbed in after them. The lid closed; the moment of complete darkness followed. Then the darkness changed slightly. Jai realized he was seeing light through the cracked chest lid in Nexhoath Nine. There was a bit of a squash as Kitty and Roughly shifted into human shape. The lid flew open.

Jai recognized the smell of the house immediately. It was extraordinary that the houses in the parallel worlds could be so similar and yet so different. The same winter sunshine spread through the hall from the windows on either side of the front door, but the house in the ninth world had an air of sadness and gloom—and that strange smell that he couldn't remember having noticed anywhere else but here.

He climbed out. Kitty followed, smoothing down her

apron and picking up the feather duster, which was still lying on the floor where she had dropped it the night before. Roughly came out of the chest, stretching his good arm out, then, more gingerly, the wounded one.

The door to the passage swung open, and Mrs. Frumbose marched into the hall, a tray in her hands. "There you are," she exclaimed when she saw Kitty and Roughly. "How dare you disappear like that? You left me with dinner and breakfast to prepare all on my own."

"Well, we're sorry about that," Kitty said. "It couldn't be helped."

"Sorry isn't good enough," Mrs. Frumbose snapped back. "As soon as I find replacements you can go look for another job."

"We won't be staying," Kitty said briefly.

Roughly took no notice of Mrs. Frumbose at all, but went to the door of the study.

"Where do you think you're going?" Mrs. Frumbose gasped.

Roughly opened the door. Kitty and Jai followed him in. Mrs. Frumbose came after them, still expostulating.

An ancient-looking Mr. Drake sat at his desk. And in front of him stood Seal.

Her head was thrown back, and she was gazing straight at the headmaster. The two of them appeared frozen, as though they had reached some kind of impasse. Mr. Drake held the object Seal had described to Jai. Its single glass eye seemed to be seeking out her soul.

Jai looked swiftly around the study. The black cards Seal had told him about were lying loose on the desk or stacked in special boxes, made of something that resembled glass, except that the boxes were molded, unlike any glass he had ever known. Also on the desk was the little thing like a suitcase. He moved to the side of the desk to see it better. It was open, showing a pearly-gray picture inside a frame. A moving picture, like nothing he had seen in his life. Little figures floated across the frame, like magic. He screwed up his eyes trying to make them out, his heart beating faster with excitement and terror.

Roughly snarled. Kitty yowled. Mrs. Frumbose pushed past them and put the tray on the desk.

"As you can see," she said tartly, "Roughly and Kitty are back now. But I've given them notice. The coffee's probably cold, but I've got my hands full with running the school. No one's done anything about lunch, and I've run out of bread and butter."

Mr. Drake frowned as this mundane speech distracted him from Seal. He swung his bony head toward Mrs. Frumbose. "Leave us," he said briefly.

As if suddenly released, Seal looked away from him. She began to speak as if she had been interrupted earlier in the middle of a sentence. ". . . not going to let you steal anything from me! I'm going to make you set Hugo free and all the others, too!"

Her face softened as she noticed Jai, Kitty, and Roughly alongside her.

Mr. Drake sneered. He was quivering, and his eyes glinted as they surveyed the four people in front of him. "So you're involved in this, too," he said. "I should have guessed. The *dog* barking, Roughly, your unpleasant voice, *Kitty*. It's clear to me now what you really are. You are from the eighth world! It was very foolhardy of you to try to operate right under my nose. You shouldn't be surprised that it backfired." He took something out of his pocket and held it between his fingers.

Kitty and Roughly went still.

"Perhaps Jai knows what this is?" Mr. Drake said, looking straight at him. "Kitty and Roughly have been very interested in you, Jai, haven't they? Offering you your own bedroom, making you special treats, always watching you. You think I didn't notice? Are you somehow connected with this ring, Jai? Do you recognize it?"

"I recognize it," Seal said loudly. "That's mine. I gave it to Hugo, and you stole it from him. Give it back."

"If you had known what it was, you never would have given it away," Mr. Drake said. "Isn't that right, Roughly?"

"What is it?" Jai whispered to Kitty.

"It's the baby's teething ring," she replied. "If only we'd known Seal had it. But the one time I saw it, you were holding it."

"I don't know much about your archaic world," Mr.

Drake sneered, "but I suspect this is a bit more than a baby's toy. In my experience these primitive objects contain a great deal of power. Is it the power that holds the door open? Does it give me the power to close your world off to you?"

Jai, watching Kitty, saw her face change as if she knew Mr. Drake was getting close to the truth and it frightened her. He moved a little closer to her side.

Seal was staring at the ring in Mr. Drake's hands. Her face lightened as if something had just dawned on her. She raised her eyes to his and smiled.

"Well, never mind," Mr. Drake said, a little disconcerted by the smile. "Plenty of time to find out. Just one or two other small matters to deal with first. Now, where was I? So the ring is yours, Celia? I think that makes your future all the more interesting to me."

Kitty stepped quickly in front of Seal. Seal gently pushed her aside and spoke without taking her eyes off Mr. Drake. "Just say yes or no, Kitty. Am I the one you were looking for?"

"Yes," Kitty breathed almost soundlessly.

"Go back to where you came from," Roughly broke out, snarling at Mr. Drake. "We don't mind what you do in your own world."

"It's none of your business what I do here, either!" Mr. Drake replied. "You have no power in this world. But I do intend to return to where I came from. And then you will have no power at all." He gave a small, chilly smile. "You are just animals," he said. "And when I go and take the key and its owner with me, your world will be closed to you. But open to me, and completely in my power."

Seal and Roughly lunged for the ring, together. They almost reached it, but Roughly was hampered by his injury, and Seal was too short.

Mr. Drake twisted the ring away and slipped it back into his pocket. His hands were shaking, and Jai thought his face was growing yellower by the minute.

"I can't let you destroy what I've set up here," the headmaster said. "You do understand, don't you? It's a matter of my own survival, you see. I need the children. I need their futures. The picture is nearly complete. And when it is, I will be immortal."

Mr. Drake picked up the black object and aimed it again at Seal.

Jai had been keeping an eye on the gray picture in the frame. It had shimmered warningly a couple of times. Now it abruptly turned black.

Mr. Drake flung the glass-eyed object down with an expression of rage and pressed several times heavily on the suitcase. It made no response.

"Infernal damnation!" he exclaimed. "No power, no power!"

He closed the lid of the suitcase and stood up, grabbed Seal by the hand, and pulled her toward the door. "I'll just have to take you with me."

His fingers were like a vise. Seal struggled and kicked in vain.

Mr. Drake grinned triumphantly at Kitty and Roughly. "I don't think you can stop me if I have the child and the ring, can you?" He opened the door and dragged Seal out into the hall.

Jai hurled himself at Mr. Drake, but the headmaster pushed him effortlessly aside.

"You're nothing special, Jai," he sneered as he lifted the lid of the chest. "Just a very ordinary little boy after all. I knew it as soon as I saw you. Still, I'll need your future and I'll be back for it."

He threw Seal into the chest and jumped in after her, pulling the lid closed.

Within a second Roughly had leaped to the chest and opened it.

It was empty.

"Where've they gone?" Jai stammered. "Back to where we went? Back to your world?"

"Only if Seal managed to get in touch with her powers very quickly," Roughly said despairingly.

"She's had no training at all," Kitty wailed.

"She shifted shape without training," Roughly reminded her. "But I don't think there's much hope. Drake will have taken her in the other direction, to the tenth world of Nexhoath."

Kitty's face turned pale. For the first time since Jai had

known her, she looked unsure of what to do.

"Then we have to follow her," she said uneasily.

"We mustn't waste any time," Roughly agreed, and began to step into the chest.

"We'll be animals there," Kitty said, "with no speech and no powers."

"We'll be animals soon enough if we stay here," Roughly said, "and with no way back to the eighth world. Come on."

Kitty took Jai's hand and squeezed it briefly. "Good-bye," she said. "Don't stay here. Run away. Do anything, but don't be here when Mr. Drake comes back."

"Why don't I come with you?" he exclaimed. "I might be able to help you."

"No. The ninth world is your world. Stay in it. But leave Nexhoath."

Roughly pulled the lid shut. There was silence in the hall. In the distance Jai could hear Mr. Corio explaining Pythagoras's theorem very loudly. Jai knew it by heart. He found himself repeating it under his breath: "In any right-angled triangle the square of the length of the hypotenuse is the sum of the square of the lengths of the two remaining sides." He almost wished he was sitting in the classroom studying math, but he knew he couldn't face the identical children and the cruel teachers. He would be the only one left no longer in school uniform, the last child at Nexhoath still free.

Kitty was right. He should run away. But where would he run to?

He looked around the hall. It was empty, but he felt as if someone was watching him, as if the eyes in the large portrait were following his every move. To get away from their gaze he stepped into Mr. Drake's study.

The black cards were still stacked on the table. Jai picked one up and looked at it, holding it carefully as if it might burn him.

It was thicker than he had at first thought. The black was slightly shiny, like a piece of coal beaten flat. At one end was a silver rectangle, and in the middle a silver disk, not set firmly into the black stuff, but loose, almost wobbly. He had never seen anything remotely like it in his life.

On one side was a white label. Someone had written on it FERN ANSPACH and the date of the day before yesterday. He put the card down carefully and picked up another one. This had Hugo's name on it. Jai held it with the utmost care, wondering what part of Hugo it contained. He shivered. He looked at the cards in the nonglass boxes. Here the labels were dated from the previous year: CHRISTOPHER PORTEOUS, he read, PAULA ARKADY, DAPHNE FRUMBOSE.

So even the teachers and the matron had been taken over by Mr. Drake. Jai tried to imagine Mrs. Frumbose as a different woman, with her own hopes and dreams. Instead she had ended up trapped at Nexhoath, her future stolen and stored on a black card.

There was a knock on the door, and Mrs. Frumbose herself walked in. She looked at the untouched tray in surprise.

"Mr. Drake didn't have his coffee," she said. Jai didn't say anything. He looked at her and saw she was like a ghost, a copy of a real person. She acted out the role of a human being, but there was no life to her, no spirit. He shuddered.

"You should be in class," she said to him. "Run along now."

"Mr. Drake told me to wait for him here," he invented quickly.

"Sit outside in the hall, then," she said in her icy voice. "I suppose that worthless Kitty and her fancy man have left." She pushed Jai out of the room and went toward the kitchen, grumbling loudly about servants.

Jai sat down on one of the uncomfortable gilt chairs in the hall. He stared at the chest. At any moment now Mr. Drake might come leaping out of it, and that would mean he would never see Seal or Kitty or Roughly again. Mr. Drake would steal something from him, the thing that made him Jai Kala, different from anyone else in any of the worlds. What would it feel like? Would he forget everything about his past—his parents and his life before he came to Nexhoath, Seal and Hugo's friendship, the strange beauty of the Clumps, how it had felt to walk over the roof with the cat, the mysterious eighth world? Would all of this be lost?

The worst thought, the one that kept coming back to him, was that if Kitty and Roughly hadn't made the mistake they did, Mr. Drake would have taken him over already. The oddity must have been at work to save him. But now, when

Mr. Drake came back, there would be no one else's future to steal except Jai's.

He felt eyes on him again and glanced up at the portrait. The figure looked more finished now, all the shadows filled in. Except one. There was one black patch just under the right cheekbone. Jai put his hand up and felt his own face. Mr. Drake had said the picture was nearly completed. Did he mean this picture? Was this where everyone ended up? Was that empty space waiting for him? Mr. Porteous's eyes, Hugo's mouth, Miss Arkady's hands all seemed to confirm his fear, and to call to him for help.

Jai jumped to his feet. He knew Kitty was right. He should open the front door and run down the driveway now, before Mr. Drake came back, while he still had the chance. But he couldn't stop thinking about the others. What would happen to them? What would happen to the eighth world? Seal was supposed to hold it together. If Seal couldn't get back there, what would happen? And what would happen to Kitty and Roughly in Mr. Drake's world? They would be animals there—and hadn't Kitty called the tenth world a hell for animals?

I can't do anything, he told himself. *I'm nobody special. I don't have the powers they have.*

Then he remembered how he had walked on the parapet of the house, as if he were flying. Kitty had taught him things because she had thought he was special, and he had learned from her. Since then he had been through the gateway between the worlds. Who knew what extra powers that had given him? He was not going to sit and wait for Mr. Drake to come back to get him. Deep down he knew what he had to do.

"It's the oddity," he said to himself in some surprise. "I can feel it. I'm bound up with Seal and Kitty and Roughly because of the oddity."

He jumped up quickly and opened the chest again. Before he could change his mind, he slid inside and closed the lid.

EIGHTEEN

Seal didn't have time to feel afraid. Mr. Drake dragged her into the chest, hitting her head on the side and pulling painfully at her hair, but none of it seemed to matter. She could only think of what she had just discovered about herself.

She wasn't an orphan misfit whom no one cared about, after all. She belonged to another world, a world whose every being loved and needed her. Kitty's quiet *yes* echoed in her mind like a trumpet call. It made her feel as if she could do anything.

Mr. Drake opened the lid of the chest and, still holding Seal firmly by the wrist, stepped out, pulling her after him.

I can change, Seal thought rapidly. I can escape him by changing. But not into a horse this time—too big; I'd be trapped in the hall. Something that can hide . . .

Think small, she told herself, think *mouse*, and she felt a surge of power swirl through her. She shrank out of Mr. Drake's grasp.

Mr. Drake gave a shout of frustration. He grabbed at her in vain as she slithered to the floor. His huge foot tried to stamp on her. She raced to the passage door and slid neatly under it.

Moving with astonishing speed, Mr. Drake opened the door and followed her.

There was a hole in the floorboards. Seal dropped into it, panting, feeling as if her heart were bursting through her skin and her eyes were bulging out of her head. But she couldn't help laughing, a little squeaky mouse laugh.

She heard Mr. Drake's footsteps overhead going toward the back of the house. Then there was silence.

She cleaned her whiskers and thought about what to do next.

There were other people in the house: She could hear voices from time to time, but she did not hear Mr. Drake's voice. Perhaps he didn't want anyone to know he was there. She decided to look for him.

But being a mouse had disadvantages. It took such a long time to get anywhere, and it was exhausting. By the time she had crept under the floorboards as far as the kitchen, she was worn out and starving hungry, too. She was afraid to eat anything because she remembered her aunt—"Not my real aunt at all, I always knew that," Seal said to herself triumphantly—used to lay poison for mice, and she didn't know what was safe to eat and what wasn't.

The kitchen was full of unfamiliar but mouthwatering smells. Seal thought she would die of hunger. Light glimmered above her from another mousehole. She ran through it and found herself just above the back steps. The door was ajar. She slipped out into the yard.

There didn't seem to be anything safe to eat there, either. She thought hungrily of the porridge that she'd had for breakfast in the eighth world. The yard looked vast to her little mouse eyes. She turned her head this way and that, listening. She sniffed the air.

She heard a tiny sound. She'd heard something like it before. A little click, like someone opening a box or a suitcase . . .

Above her head was a small round window. Seal tried to remember which room in Nexhoath it belonged to. A little room, like a storeroom, not far from the kitchen. It must be the housekeeper's sitting room that she'd visited with Jai. And the more she listened, the more sure she was that there was someone in the sitting room, someone who didn't want to be heard, who was trying to be very quiet, but who couldn't help making tiny noises that only a mouse would hear.

The trouble was, a mouse couldn't see into the room. The window was too high, and the stones of the wall too smooth. Seal took a deep breath and thought herself back into human form.

She was crouching near the kitchen door, the windowsill just above her head. She stood up carefully and peered into the room.

Mr. Drake was there with his suitcase. He had tied it to the wall with a long piece of cord. Seal peered at it, puzzled, trying to make out what he was doing with it, what it was.

Mr. Drake took off his black frock coat and tight black trousers, dropping them on the floor. He shook out his shirttails and scratched himself. He looked repulsive with his bony, hairy legs poking out of his undershorts. He opened the cupboard and took out a long loose garment like a nightshirt, and a white wig. He climbed into the nightshirt, buttoned it up, and put on the wig, tying a yellow headband around his forehead.

He picked up the trousers and felt in the pocket. He took out the bone ring. He held it up for a few moments, gloating. Then he tied a piece of string to it and hung it around his neck, under the nightshirt.

I'll get that back, Seal promised herself.

At that moment Mr. Drake looked up, and their eyes met. His mouth formed a shape of surprise and pleasure. He adjusted his nightshirt, left the suitcase where it was, and walked swiftly toward the door.

Seal ran across the yard, thinking *speed.* She felt herself change, without really planning to. She felt the power and strength of the horse envelop her. Grateful, because it was something familiar, she trotted behind the barn toward the paddock.

There was one gray horse there, almost completely white with age, like Moonlight. He whinnied when he heard the sound of hooves, and Seal whinnied back. The fence had lost a rail in one corner, and it was easy for her to jump over.

She and the gray snorted at each other, but the gray was too old to bother much about strange happenings. He was just happy to have the company of another horse. He put his head down to eat and Seal did the same, watching the house all the time.

The grass in the paddock was thin and unsatisfying. And there was something wrong with the air in this world. It made her eyes ache and water. Lifting her head Seal peered toward the Clumps. They weren't there. Houses covered the hillside. She listened for the clack of the mill, the babble of the stream, but there was no sound of them. Instead, a dull constant roar came from the end of the driveway. Vehicles that she thought must be cars tore past at unbelievable speeds, quite unlike the sedate steam-powered cars of the ninth world.

She shuddered, as if flies were crawling on her, and her long brown tail flicked nervously. Her ears lay flat on her head. She felt like kicking out against this alien place. She hated it.

This was what the eighth world might become if Mr. Drake and others like him gained access to it. She had to get back her ring and stop him. But she had no idea how she was going to do it.

After a few moments, Mr. Drake walked around the side of the house from the front garden. His hands were folded together, and he walked with great gravity, his head bowed.

But Seal was aware of his eyes, darting in every direction. He was searching for her.

The temptation to shift shape and flee was almost overwhelming. But she had to stay near the house and she must not give herself away. Think horse, think horse, she told herself, and her human self retreated further and further, until she was simply a horse, grazing in the paddock beside the old gray.

Mr. Drake took one last look around and then went into the house, through the kitchen door.

Seal followed the old horse. When he moved, she moved. When he looked up at the horizon, she looked. And when he pricked his ears and moved toward the fence to investigate a movement in the yard, she did the same thing.

The old horse blew out through his nostrils and then trotted away to the end of the paddock. He turned to stare again.

He must have seen a dog, Seal thought, staring, too.

Roughly limped slowly into the yard. A few seconds later, Kitty slid like a shadow around the corner of the house. The two animals looked this way and that, and then went to the trough near the paddock gate, to drink. They gave the horses a brief glance and lay down near the trough, waiting.

Seal wasn't sure if they had recognized her or not. She didn't dare call out to them, in case Mr. Drake was watching. Despite the danger she knew they were in in the tenth world, she was glad they had followed her. At least she was not alone.

Several people drifted through the yard from the front garden, most of them, like Mr. Drake, moving gravely and quietly with hands folded and eyes lowered. They came and went. The animals—the old horse and Seal in the paddock, Roughly and Kitty alongside the trough—took little notice of them.

The screen door from the kitchen opened with a thump, and two people came out arguing. One was a man, wearing a navy blue jacket and blue trousers with holes in the knees. He had shoulder-length yellowish hair and a wispy beard. The other was a woman in a long flowing pale mauve dress, with a gray tasseled shawl around her shoulders. The woman was carrying a baby.

They had an impassioned conversation as they walked toward the paddock. The old gray horse ambled toward them, and Seal followed, listening carefully.

"There's another horse there now! A bay horse! Did you rescue that one, too?" demanded the woman.

"Wow!" said the man, stroking first the gray and then Seal. "That is totally unreal!"

"Moon Unit, we can't keep all these animals! We haven't got any money! It's wrong to keep them if you can't look after them. I've been to the council, and they're going to come to look at the horse and make arrangements to take it away."

"Take it to the slaughterhouse," Moon Unit said gloomily. "To the glue factory!"

"You aren't allowed to keep horses here, anyway," the woman said. "It's against council regulations. Where did the second horse come from?"

"I honestly don't know, Lightfoot! It's just appeared. I did not bring it here."

Lightfoot turned away from him in exasperation and immediately noticed Roughly.

"There's a dog, too! And a cat over there as well. Did you bring them here?"

"No, I've never seen them before. They must be strays." Moon Unit held his hand out to Roughly. "Here, boy, good dog."

Roughly's tail wagged briefly.

"Couldn't we keep them?" Moon Unit pleaded. "It's good for the kids to have pets around. Might drag Leaf away from the computer."

"We can't afford to keep them. We've got no money to buy food. The phone's been cut off. The electricity will go next. And there's nothing left to eat except some rice and carrots."

"Carrots and rice make a good meal," Moon Unit replied.

"It's not enough for growing children."

Moon Unit took the baby and clucked at her. "Nothing wrong with Lila," he said. "She's as healthy as anything."

Lightfoot looked as if she was getting angrier and angrier, but they were interrupted by the sound of a van coming up the driveway. It had writing on the side that read, NEXHOATH CITY COUNCIL POUND. It stopped in a swirl of gravel, and Lightfoot hurried toward it.

"Another horse has turned up now. And a dog and a cat. I think people just dump them here," she said as the driver got out. He was wearing a brown and green uniform and a broad-brimmed hat, and he carried a net in his hand.

"If they've got no collars or registration, then you're probably right," he agreed. Without hesitating, he walked straight to Roughly and threw the net over him, before the dog had time to move. It was all done efficiently and skillfully, as if he had caught many dogs before. In less than a minute, Roughly was tied up in the back of the van. His eyes were furious, and he was snarling through the net, but he was helpless.

"Cats are harder," the man said. "May have to come back with a trap for it."

Kitty seemed to be torn between staying with Roughly and not leaving Nexhoath. Her eyes darted to and fro in anguish. She ran a little way toward the barn, and then ran back again, meowing loudly. Lightfoot grabbed her and gave her to the man. He shut her in a box, placed it in the van, and climbed back into the driver's seat.

"I'll come back with a truck for the horses," he called. "Sometime tomorrow, it'll be."

Lightfoot waved at him and started to walk toward the house. "You look after Lila for a while," she called to Moon Unit. "I'm going to meditate. My psychic centers are all confused."

Moon Unit held the baby up so she could see the horses. She laughed and wriggled.

"Nice horsey, nice horsey!" Moon Unit crooned.

Nice was the last thing Seal felt. She watched the van disappear with a sinking heart. It was because of her that Kitty and Roughly had come to this world. What would happen to them, and how could she rescue them?

Nineteen

Holding his breath, Jai lifted the chest lid. He wasn't sure where he would be, or what opened the gateway into the tenth world of Nexhoath, but it seemed as if he already had new powers. The gateway had opened for him as it had for the others. He was definitely no longer in Nexhoath Nine.

The hall was almost unrecognizable. There were no portraits. Instead, one wall was painted orange, and another had a mural of a forest on it, with twisting vines and snakes hidden among the leaves. There was a heavy, musky smell, rather like the incense Jai's mother used to burn.

The house was very cold. The wind was whistling under the front door and through several broken panes in the skylight. The chandelier had lost most of its crystal droplets. Those that remained were dirty and stained. A few of the lamps were alight, but they weren't candles. No candle could have stayed alight in that draft. Jai had no idea what they were.

Around the front door someone had written a lot of swirly words in black paint. LOVE. PEACE. THE MAGIC DRAGON RULES THE WORLD. SAVE THE WHALES. RESPECT THE LEY LINES.

Apart from the chest there was no furniture at all in the

hall, but from the frame around the central skylight a pyramid shape was suspended. A young woman was sitting underneath it with her legs crossed beneath her in what looked like a very uncomfortable position. She was wearing a pale mauve dress and a tasseled shawl, and her hair was very long and braided in a single plait.

Jai let the lid fall until he could just peep through a crack. He watched the woman for a few moments. She didn't move. Her eyes were closed, and she was vibrating slightly, as if she were humming. She seemed to be quite distant. He thought he could get out of the chest without her noticing him.

Trying not to make the slightest sound, he pushed up the lid and climbed out.

The woman spoke without turning her head. "Hello! If you're looking for Leaf, he's in the computer room."

Jai gulped and said, "Thank you," very politely. He had no idea who or even what Leaf might be, or where the computer room was, but he was relieved the woman didn't ask him who he was and what he was doing. He didn't particularly want her to see him. He was sure his clothes, his hair, himself, *everything* looked wrong in this world. Edging away from her he opened a door and backed into what, in the ninth world, was Mr. Drake's study.

A series of small explosions behind him made him jump and spin around. He remembered the noise of Mr. Porteous's gun, the red blossoming on the dog's shoulder.

Colors were blossoming in front of his eyes, flowers of red, yellow, and orange, but they were coming from a sort of box on a table. A boy about his age was sitting in front of it, his eyes glued to the pictures on it, moving pictures that Jai recognized instantly—they were more or less like those in Mr. Drake's suitcase.

The room had the same mysterious smell as Mr. Drake's study, and on the table were black and gray cards, just like the ones on the headmaster's desk. Jai felt giddy with excitement. Mr. Drake's tools were right here in front of him.

"Do you mind telling me what you're doing?" he said.

The boy jumped slightly and looked up. The picture made more colored flowers, and the box played noisy music.

"Hey," the boy said, "now I'm dead! Have to start again." He sounded quite cheerful about it. He looked very cheerful, with bright brown eyes almost hidden under jaggedly cut hair, and big, slightly uneven white teeth that gave him an attractive grin.

"What is that?" Jai persisted. He realized the boy would probably think he was a complete idiot, but he didn't care. He had to find out how this machine or invention or magic box or whatever it was worked.

"It's a computer," the boy replied airily. "Don't your olds let you have one? My dad doesn't like me playing games on it, he is so out of it."

"How does it work?"

"Well, you plug it in, and you turn it on, and you use this

thing, it's called a mouse. . . ." The boy spoke slowly as if he did indeed think Jai was a half-wit.

"Plug it in?" Jai looked at the gray cord that connected the computer to the wall. "What does it plug into?"

The boy stared at Jai. "Where've you come from? The back blocks? Were you living out in one of those funny communes where they don't believe in electricity or cars or anything? Dad wanted us to go and join one, but luckily Mom put her foot down."

"Yes, sort of," Jai said. "I just don't know much about elec . . ." He stumbled over the unfamiliar word.

"Electricity. Weird." The boy stared at Jai for a few moments. Then he grinned his lopsided grin. "I'm Leaf."

"Jai."

"Sit down. I'll show you how the computer works."

It was a revelation to Jai. He couldn't believe anyone could have invented something so clever. All the sums and the puzzles and the math problems that he spent so much time on inside his head—they were the work of an instant to the computer. He gathered from Leaf that there was nothing intrinsically dangerous about it. It was just a system. Mr. Drake must have extra powers, probably from another world, that he exploited to steal some vital part of people and store it in the portrait.

Hugo and Seal had told him Mr. Drake was a drackle. Jai had never really believed in drackles, but he knew they were supposed to be able to suck out people's souls, having no souls of their own. If a drackle came from another world, it might have even more sinister powers. Mr. Drake combined these with the computer system. No one in the ninth world could resist him.

And the system needed electricity, although Jai was still not sure what that was or how it worked. But people used electricity as a source of power in this world, which explained the lamps and the computer, whereas in his world they used water and steam.

"Can this computer run without electricity?" he asked Leaf. "Could you take it somewhere where there was no electricity and still use it?"

"Not this one," Leaf said. "This is called a desktop. But you can get portable ones, laptops. They run on batteries, which you have to recharge by plugging the computer into a power point."

Jai smiled. *No power, no power,* Mr. Drake had said. Now he understood why. "How long does it take to recharge?"

"A few hours, I guess. There's an old fart here called Babaji. He's got one. He's always leaving it in the little room next to the kitchen to recharge. He thinks Mom and Dad don't notice. Well, they don't. But I do!"

Jai went pink. He couldn't believe Leaf would use a rude word so casually. Especially not in connection with *babaji,* which he knew was a Hindi term of affection and respect. All the same he repeated it to himself under his breath. He liked

Leaf, liked the way he was so cheerful and irreverent. He didn't think Leaf would ever put on a school uniform and become like everyone else.

Then the meaning of Leaf's words sank in. So Mr. Drake had to keep returning to the tenth world to recharge his computer. And then to the ninth world to recharge himself, to keep adding to the picture. . . .

All this reassured him somewhat. He had thought Mr. Drake had invincible magic powers, but at least some of those powers were not magic. They were ordinary skills that could be used and controlled by children, in the tenth world, anyway.

"I'll show you something else," Leaf said. "Look, you can put pictures into the computer. This is a scanner, and here's a photo of me."

Jai picked up the picture and looked at it. "What an amazing likeness! Who painted it? Your father?"

Leaf frowned. "No one painted it. It's a photo. Photograph? With a camera?"

Jai shook his head and shrugged.

"Gee, where did you come from, man? You are like positively primitive!" Leaf passed the thing he'd called a scanner over the photo, and it appeared, as if by magic, on the big picture that Jai had learned was called a screen.

"Are you in the machine now?"

Leaf grinned. "No! No way!" He pressed a few keys, and the picture broke up into sections. Leaf moved them around, putting his feet where his head should be. "You can make a game out of it, try to put the picture back together again."

The sections of the photo now looked more and more like the portrait in the hall in Nexhoath Nine. Jai gazed at it, fascinated. It was so like what he suspected Mr. Drake did. Except the headmaster collected parts of different people and put them together to make one big picture. And in that big picture lay the drackle's life.

"You aren't caught in there somehow?"

"I told you. No way!" Leaf laughed as if it was a huge joke.

"No part of you?" Jai persisted.

"It hasn't stolen my soul, if that's what you mean."

That was exactly what Jai did mean. Mr. Drake could do something extra that did steal the soul. "How do you get the picture out again?"

Leaf showed him how to press a key for "delete," and section by section the boy's face vanished from the screen. Jai looked sideways at him. He was still grinning, still cheerful. Nothing had happened to him.

"Hey," Leaf said, "I bet you've never seen television, either, have you?"

Jai shook his head.

"It's like photos, but moving. It's pretty cool. Something else my dad hates, though. Come on, I'll show you."

Jai was so fascinated by the computer, he agreed

instantly. Leaf pressed a key, and the screen went blank. The two boys got up and walked through the hall.

"Hey, Mom!" Leaf said to the woman who was still sitting under the pyramid.

"Hey, Leaf," she replied without opening her eyes. "Your friend find you?"

"Yup. How are your chakras? All nicely opened up?"

The woman did not reply. Leaf rolled his eyes at Jai and led him through a green baize door, into the kitchen.

It was far messier than Kitty's kitchen, but much warmer than the rest of the house. In the middle of the room was a baby's cot, with a brightly colored mobile of stars swinging above it. There were several old couches in the corners, and in front of one of these was another, larger box. Leaf pressed a button on it, and it burst into life. More moving pictures flickered across it. Jai had to squint to see them clearly. A funny-looking cat was stalking a mouse. The cat jumped, the mouse dropped something on it and squashed it flat. Leaf laughed loudly. Jai was entranced.

From outside came the sound of quick steps. A man walked into the kitchen. His hair was long and yellowish, and he had a wispy beard. He was carrying a plump baby of about nine months old who was alternately playing with the leather thong the man wore around his neck and rubbing her eyes sleepily.

"Guess what, Leaf," the man said as he passed the boy. "Another horse has turned up in the paddock. Go have a look." Then he bent over the cot, gently loosened the thong from the baby's grip, and laid her down.

"When this is finished, Dad," Leaf said. "Jai wanted to watch television."

"Hi, Jai," Leaf's father said. "Are your folks doing the meditation class with Babaji?"

Jai made a noncommittal noise.

"Turn the TV off, Leaf. Lila wants her nap."

"Lila likes TV," Leaf replied.

Someone walked past the window.

"Here comes Babaji now," Leaf's father said. "They must be taking a break. I'll put the jug on."

Jai caught only the briefest glimpse of the figure walking past the window, but it was enough. Despite the white hair and the long white nightshirt garment, he knew at once that Babaji was Mr. Drake.

Almost without thinking, he made a dash for the pantry.

"Hang on," Leaf said. "Where you going?"

The kitchen door opened as Jai pulled the pantry door shut behind him. He dived down into the secret passage, found his way through the darkness, and came up in the barn. He was shaking. It wasn't only the sight of Mr. Drake, or this unnerving world—like, yet so unlike, his own. He was furious. How dare Mr. Drake impersonate a holy man? What an insult to call himself Babaji. Leaf was right. He was an old fart. He had to be stopped. He had to be destroyed.

Jai had never felt so angry in his life. The anger helped

him to not be afraid. He went stealthily to the barn door and looked out toward the Clumps.

The Clumps were not there. The hill was covered with houses, all very alike, and all with neat gardens. Jai slipped out of the barn and around toward the back of Nexhoath. He could now see that the old mansion was almost completely surrounded by houses. The fields and woods of his own world had disappeared. There was just one scrubby paddock left, where two horses grazed side by side.

The bay would be Midnight, Jai thought, and the gray Moonlight or Starlight. He wondered what had happened to the other gray.

A terrible noise echoed through the sky, and he threw himself to the ground. Something huge flew over his head, so low that the windows rattled. It made one of the horses in the paddock start and shy, too. The bay horse put its head down and galloped the length of the paddock and back again. The gray horse kept on eating.

When the noise had faded a little, Jai got to his feet and looked up. A huge object with wings was rising into the sky. It must be a flying machine. He'd always thought they only happened in stories. Now he'd seen one for himself. He found himself thinking his father would never believe him. Then he wondered if he ever would see his father again. He probably wouldn't unless he worked out how to defeat Mr. Drake. Where were Kitty and Roughly? Where was Seal? He wished he hadn't wasted time watching the television with

Leaf. He had to find the others without Mr. Drake finding him.

He called quietly, "Kitty! Roughly!" Then he walked back around the other side of the barn and called again, more loudly.

"What's up, man?" Leaf's father was standing on the back step, watching him. "How did you get out here?" he went on curiously. "Leaf was wondering where you'd shot off to." Jai stood still, not knowing what to reply, not sure if he should make a run for it.

The man drifted toward him and held out a hand. "I'm Martin, known as Moon Unit. Leaf's dad, you probably guessed. I'm in charge of this place, the Rainbow Commune and Meditation Center. You lost a dog and a cat, by any chance?"

Jai nodded. "Yes, I have. Kitty and Roughly, they're called."

Moon Unit made a distressed sound. "That's too bad. They've gone to the pound. The dogcatcher was here earlier. Man, I'm sorry. I told Lightfoot we should have kept them."

"How do I get them back?" Jai demanded.

"Uh. I dunno, man." Moon Unit stroked his wispy beard. "Could try the phone. Phone the council. Yeah, that's the thing to do. Wait here. I'll go phone the council."

He drifted back to the house and disappeared inside. After a few moments he returned shaking his head. "Bummer, man, I forgot, phone's dead. Guess no one paid the bill. Sorry."

It meant nothing to Jai. What on earth was a phone? And

what happened when it was dead? Moon Unit didn't seem too appalled, so perhaps it wasn't really a disaster.

"Thanks, anyway," Jai said. "Where is the council? I'd better try to go there."

Moon Unit seemed to be thinking hard. "I'll take you," he said finally.

"Is that all right?" Jai said. "That would be wonderful."

"Yeah, it's cool, man. It's the least I can do. I feel so bad, letting your animals go to the pound. Going to the unemployment office, anyway; gotta drop in my benefit form. Come on."

He set off toward the yard. Jai followed, wondering what unemployment office and benefit form meant. The bay horse neighed loudly as they went past.

"Weird," Moon Unit said. "I put one horse in there the other day. The gray one. Someone abandoned it. Then the other one suddenly appeared this morning. Like it materialized. Out of the ether! Unreal!"

Jai turned and looked at the horse. There was something familiar about it. He went up to the fence and stroked its nose.

"You like horses?" Moon Unit said. "Wish Leaf did. He doesn't like anything except computers and television. Television's dead rubbish, man. A horse is a beautiful living thing."

"Jai," the horse whispered, "don't jump. It's me, Seal."

"Seal," he said in relief, and laid his cheek against the horse's huge one.

"What can we do?" Seal breathed. "Kitty and Roughly

have been taken away, and Mr. Drake is here. He's walking around in a white wig and a nightshirt. What's he up to?"

"He's waiting for his computer to recharge and pretending to be a holy man," Jai replied. "I haven't got time to explain it all, but I know how he steals people's futures. At least, I know some of it. I'm going to try to get Kitty and Roughly. This man's called Moon Unit. I've been talking to his son. They're nice people. Moon Unit's going to help me find the animals. Mr. Drake can't move for a little while."

Seal shook her big horse head. "I don't understand much of that, Jai, but I trust you. What shall I do?"

"He mustn't get hold of you. If he has the ring and you, he's got all the power. But if you could get the ring . . ."

"I'll see what I can do." Seal neighed softly.

Jai gave her one last pat and walked away, looking back at her over his shoulder.

"Wow," Moon Unit breathed quietly. "That was beautiful. I swear that horse was talking to you. That was the coolest thing I ever saw." Shaking his head, he led the way to the van.

It was painted yellow with blue and red flowers, and at the front was a small sign that said vw. Inside it was full of rubbish. Two mice ran under the seat when Moon Unit opened the door, and he had to clear several cans and cartons from the passenger seat before Jai could sit down.

The van took a while to start up, but once Moon Unit

had chanted a few strange sounds to it, the engine obediently burst into noisy life. They rattled down the driveway. Jai turned to look back at the house. He remembered how he had first seen Nexhoath Nine, in the car with his parents. It looked so different here, surrounded by hundreds of houses, shorn of its grandeur.

At the gate a colorful hand-painted sign read: RAINBOW COMMUNE. Over it someone had scrawled: KILL A HIPPIE and DRUGGIES OUT. Next to it was a larger billboard that announced FOR SALE. HUGE CENTRALLY LOCATED SITE. GREAT DEVELOPMENT POTENTIAL.

Moon Unit saw Jai looking at the billboard and said with unusual vigor, "They want to pull down the old house for development. They're trying to kick us out. But we won't leave, no way. That house is a magic place. Like, it's got these really weird special vibes."

Jai nodded but didn't say anything. If only Moon Unit knew how weird and how special the vibes were.

He looked out the window. It was stuck half-open, and the glass was very dirty, but through the open bit he could study this new world. It was much more crowded than the ninth world, jam-packed with houses and cars and people. The roads were so busy that the van moved along at a crawl. Huge trucks thundered past, much bigger than anything Jai had ever seen, and every two minutes one of the flying machines roared overhead.

"In the flight path," Moon Unit shouted. "Bummer, hey?"

Jai nodded wisely again. He wondered what the cars were powered by. It obviously wasn't steam. Whatever it was gave out terrible fumes. His eyes were getting sore, and he could feel a headache starting. Also, the motion of the van was making him feel rather sick.

It seemed to take ages to get to wherever they were going. Jai started to fidget with impatience. How long would it take Mr. Drake to recharge his computer and would he then return to the ninth world and close the gateway? Or would he leave the gateway open and catch Jai and the others when they returned? *If* they returned. At this rate, by the time he had found Kitty and Roughly, Mr. Drake would have left the tenth world. If only the van would go a bit faster.

Twenty

After Jai had left with Moon Unit, Seal stood watching the house, trying to make a plan. Mr. Drake, in his holy man disguise, came out the back door with two of his disciples. They walked around to the terrace, where they stood conversing deeply.

Seal didn't want to stop being a horse. She felt safe and protected in this shape. But she knew Jai was right. She had to get the ring back, so she had to follow Mr. Drake.

Flies bothered her, making her swish her tail. They gave her an idea. She would fly around the house. That would be much easier than running like a mouse. But a fly was too small and too vulnerable. . . .

Think *flight*, think *bird*.

The bay horse shimmered, shrank, and flew into the air. The old gray horse threw his head up, startled, and then broke into a lumbering trot.

Seal fluttered her wings frantically and just avoided crashing into the horse trough. Flying was much harder than it looked. She tried to perch in a shrub and nearly poked her eyes out. She tumbled to the ground, flapped her wings again, and fluttered around onto the terrace. Mr. Drake was no longer there.

The arms had been broken off the statues, and their drapery was covered with black markings, but Seal hardly had time to notice this. She managed to perch on the head of one of the marble figures. From here she could see quite well into the dining room.

It was empty of chairs or tables. About a dozen people were sitting cross-legged on the floor with their eyes closed. Seal thought they might be praying, though it didn't look like any church she had ever seen. Mr. Drake sat with his back to the window. She half flew, half hopped across, and perched on the sill.

She cocked her little head sideways and looked upward. The fan window at the top of the casement was held open by an iron bar. Seal fluttered up and perched on it.

No one in the room moved.

She could see practically straight down Mr. Drake's neck. She saw the cord that held the ring, and as he leaned forward she saw the ring itself, dangling against his bony chest.

Mr. Drake put up his hand and scratched the back of his neck, parting the long white hair. The cord was knotted at the back, and his scaly skin was red beneath the knot, where it had been irritated.

If I could untie the knot . . . , Seal thought. But I need fingers for that. And wings to get over to him from here. And I've got to be something not very big, otherwise he'll notice me.

She hesitated, thinking how awful to be so small and so close to Mr. Drake. He would be able to squash her in an instant. Then she thought of the magic of the Clumps, as she so often had when she was unhappy at Nexhoath. She thought of the animals there, the birds and insects that she had studied and drawn. Her world, the eighth world, had that magic all the time. She wasn't going to let Mr. Drake destroy it. The animal world would help her.

She shifted shape into a praying mantis, and flew toward the back of Mr. Drake's neck.

It was like landing in an arid desert, full of craters and tough white hairs. Luckily Mr. Drake's wig gave her a certain amount of protection. He couldn't feel her through it. With her tough jaws and agile front legs, she alternately pulled and tugged and bit at the knot. Once Mr. Drake put his hand up to scratch and swatted her two yards away, but she spread her wings in time and managed to fly back again.

Finally the knot gave way. Seal had hoped she could hook the ends of the cord over the bristly hair of the wig and that they would hold until Mr. Drake stood up. Then the ring would slip to the ground, and she would grab it and run. But the ring was too heavy. As soon as the knot was undone, it came off the cord and began to fall.

Mr. Drake made a grab at it, but it rolled to the ground and away over the floor. Seal had only an instant to decide what to change into. Something fast enough to outrun Mr. Drake, yet small enough to get under doors if they were shut. Unless she opened them with hands as a girl again. But if she was a girl, Mr. Drake could grab her easily. And she could run faster as an animal.

Mr. Drake dashed after the ring. *Must stop him,* Seal thought. She changed into a cat and dug her claws into his neck.

He seized her in fury, struggling to pull her off. She tried to jump away, but her claws became entangled in the wig. The wig separated from his head and fell, with the cat still caught in it, to the floor.

Mr. Drake shouted and stamped. Seal wriggled and rolled. She came loose from the wig and found the ring. She grabbed it in her mouth and ran toward the door.

It opened at that moment, and Lightfoot walked in. She was carrying a small gong, to beat for the end of the session. Around her the praying people were already jumping to their feet, astonished by the noise and by the sight of Mr. Drake—Babaji—without his hair.

"Goddess on earth!" Lightfoot screamed when she saw Seal. "Another cat! Where are all these animals coming from?"

"Stop it, stop it," Mr. Drake bellowed. In a manner quite unbecoming to a holy man, he hitched up his nightshirt and ran after the cat, pushing his disciples roughly out of the way.

Seal raced through the passage toward the green baize door. She jumped at it with both her front paws, and it swung open. She slipped through the crack quickly before it could swing shut again.

Now she had to hide the ring. She gazed frantically around the kitchen. She was so tired. It was getting harder and harder to think straight. Kitty and Roughly could have told her that shape-shifting uses up enormous amounts of energy and should be practiced slowly at the start. Seal had already used up far more energy than she really had available to her. But Kitty and Roughly were not there to teach and guide her. Seal was all on her own.

A boy was sitting on a couch in the corner watching something. She hadn't time to see what it was. There was a baby's cot in the middle of the room, a baby asleep in it, her thumb in her mouth.

Seal jumped into the cot, dropped the ring, and pushed it under the pillow with her paws. The baby woke and started to cry.

She jumped out of the cot and ran to the back door. It was shut.

She mewed frantically, hoping the boy would get up and open the door. She could hear Mr. Drake's steps in the passage.

The green baize door swung open.

Twenty-one

At last Moon Unit drew up in front of a cream brick building.

"These are the council offices. You go in there and ask about your pets," he said. "I gotta go two doors down."

Jai suddenly felt terrified. He had no idea how to behave in this world, what its rules were or anything. He was sure he'd make a mess of it all.

"You couldn't come with me, could you?" he asked shyly.

"Oh." Moon Unit thought about this deeply. "Okay. Sure. That's cool. Come on. I'll get it all sorted out."

He ambled in through the imposing doors of the council offices and up to the counter. He didn't seem to be fazed by the hushed atmosphere and the stern faces that peered at him from behind glass partitions.

Jai followed him. The place reminded him of the Bureaucracy offices in the ninth world. It made him think of the places his parents had had to go to while they were trying to sort out their visas. He'd hated those places, and he hated this one, too.

A rather snappy woman asked Moon Unit what he wanted. Jai could see she was working on a computer like Leaf's, and so was everyone else in the office. That must make their work so much faster. Lights glowed in the ceiling, and the building was warm, even though there were no fires or radiators. Electricity must be the most wonderful thing.

"Were the animals registered?" the woman inquired at the end of Moon Unit's rambling explanation.

"Not exactly, probably not," Moon Unit replied after a questioning look at Jai, who assumed registration for animals was like visas for people, and shook his head.

"Try Save the Animals," she said curtly, and returned to her computer.

Moon Unit tapped on the glass. "Like, where is Save the Animals?"

She pointed to a yellow object on the wall. "Look it up."

Moon Unit made a face at her. "You should be more helpful. I'm a taxpayer, you know."

She shot an evil look at him. "I very much doubt that."

"Well, I may not be a taxpayer, but at least I'm a human being," Moon Unit mumbled as he took a huge book out from beneath the yellow thing. "Not a robot. Or a monster. Unlike some people." He flipped through the pages. "Here it is. Banfield Road, Banfield."

"What's this thing?" Jai said, touching the yellow object.

"That's a telephone," Moon Unit said. "*Tele*—far, *phone*—speak. A far speaker. Usually called *phone* for short."

"Must be very useful," Jai said. It was like the voice pipe, but it obviously had a much wider range. If only they had far speakers in the ninth world, he could speak to his parents.

"Yeah, man, it's very useful," Moon Unit replied. He put the book down and led the way back to the van. When they were both inside he gave Jai a long searching look. "Where do you come from? Is it some commune I've never heard of? I don't want to pry, man, but you just, like, don't seem to know much about things."

"I can't explain," Jai said. "I've just got to find Roughly and Kitty as quickly as possible and take them home." He began to feel the sick-making sense of urgency again.

"It's like you're from some other world." Moon Unit's eyes were huge. "That's spooky stuff!"

"Do you think we could hurry?" Jai begged him.

"Sure, sure." Moon Unit began to chant as he started up the van. "Banfield, here we come."

"It's very nice of you to take me there," Jai began, sorry he hadn't explained things better.

"It's cool, it's cool. I gotta help you. Anyway, I always wanted to meet an alien. I think that's what you are. A genuine, real live alien!"

Jai smiled to himself. He wondered if Moon Unit had ever heard of the oddity. He was sure it was linking them now.

Moon Unit picked his way carefully through the busy streets and onto something called a freeway. Despite his vagueness, he was quite a good driver. After about twenty minutes whizzing down the freeway faster than Jai had ever traveled in his life, they saw a sign that read: BANFIELD NEXT EXIT.

Banfield was a dreary suburb of small, ill-kept houses and old, run-down factories, most of which seemed to have ceased operating. Moon Unit drove slowly down Banfield Road and stopped in front of a large shedlike building. A sign at the front read: SAVE THE ANIMALS INC. LOST DOGS AND CATS HOME.

As soon as the van stopped they could hear the barking of dogs. Moon Unit, suddenly becoming very protective, led Jai into the building. The reception area was deserted, but after a few moments a door opened and a young woman came hurrying in. She was wearing trousers like Moon Unit's, made out of the same blue canvaslike material but without the holes in the knees, and a white smock with KELLY embroidered on the lapel. Her face was tired, but friendly.

"Sorry," she gasped. "I'm the only one here today and I'm trying to do everything. Have you come to buy a pet or have you lost one?"

"I've lost a cat and a dog," Jai said. "The cat is gray with white paws, and the dog is very big, with blackish, dark gray fur."

"Like a wolfhound?" Kelly interrupted. "He's here. Oh, I'm so glad he's got an owner. I was really worried about him. We aren't meant to keep those big dogs for long, you know. People don't usually want something like that. I was dreading having to put him to sleep."

When she saw Jai's face, she added gently, "I'm afraid that's what happens to most of them. We get far too many to find homes for."

"Bummer," Moon Unit muttered sadly.

"Come on," Kelly said. "We'll see if we can find your little cat, too. What's her name?"

"Kitty," Jai said.

Kelly laughed. "Very original. If I go in there calling *Kitty, Kitty, Kitty,* they'll all come running." She opened the door into a passageway, then led them through a wire door into a courtyard.

All around the courtyard were pens full of dogs and cats. When they saw the people they became almost hysterical, barking and meowing even more loudly, as if they were saying, *Is that you? Have you come to take me home? Please take me home.*

"This is so sad," Moon Unit said. "This is so heavy!"

Roughly lay in the last pen in the row, head on paws, eyes half-closed. When he spotted Jai he lifted his head, and his tail started wagging. He stood up and pushed his nose through the wire. Jai knelt and tried to pat him. "Roughly," he said. He was so pleased to see the dog that he was almost crying. He put his face close to Roughly's and whispered, "Talk to me, Roughly."

The big dog shook his head. His eyes were dark and intense with feeling, but he could not speak.

"I've got to get them out of here," Jai turned urgently to the two adults. "I've got to get them home. Where's Kitty?"

"I think that might be her," Kelly said, pointing across

the yard. A little gray cat was clawing at the wire and meowing loudly. When Jai ran to her, she purred and purred.

"There's no doubt who they belong to," Kelly said. She unlocked the cage, and Kitty leaped into Jai's arms. "Have you got a leash for the dog?"

Jai shook his head. Moon Unit untied the leather thong around his neck and held it out. "Here, use this."

Kelly gave it a rather disapproving look, but she unlocked Roughly's cage and let the dog out. "He hasn't even got a collar," she said, holding him by the scruff of the neck.

Moon Unit twisted the thong around Roughly's neck and held the ends out to Jai.

"Just hang on to him for a moment," Kelly said. "Bring them both into reception, and we'll sort out the paper-work."

There was no need to hang on to Roughly. He kept so close to Jai that when Jai stopped at the desk, Roughly bumped into him.

"He's very well trained, isn't he?" Kelly said. "Good boy, aren't you." She bent down to pat the dog. Roughly flattened his ears, looking faintly disgusted. His expression made Jai grin. He put Kitty down on top of the desk. She sat neatly and quietly, watching Kelly's every move.

"Aren't they amazing?" Kelly said. "I swear they understand every word you say." She took out a big book and her pen. "Now, I just need your name and address."

Jai shot a helpless look at Moon Unit. Moon Unit was watching Kitty and Roughly, his mind off on some track of its own. Jai tapped him on the arm.

"What's your address?" he whispered.

"Rainbow Commune, Nexhoath Hall, Nexhoath," Moon Unit replied. Then he whispered to Jai, "Are they really animals?"

Kelly was looking at them suspiciously. "Are you his dad?" she said.

"I'm his uncle," Moon Unit replied with great aplomb. "I'm looking after him while his mother's in the hospital. That must be why the animals strayed. They were, like, in a new place."

"Okay," Kelly said, writing in the book. "I guess that's fine. Now I just need the fifty dollars to cover costs."

"Fifty dollars?" Moon Unit echoed. He looked at Jai. "Do you happen to have fifty dollars on you?" he asked hopefully.

Jai shook his head.

"Bummer." Moon Unit was silent for a couple of seconds. Kelly waited, pen in hand.

"Suppose I bring it next week? When I've got my unemployment money. No? No good?"

"I'm really sorry," Kelly said. "I can't let the animals go without payment. Those are the rules. I'll keep them till you come back. They won't be in any danger."

"You don't understand," Jai said. "I've got to get them home."

"Sorry," Kelly said, and took the leather thong from Jai's hand.

Roughly let out a spine-chilling howl. For a moment there was complete silence. Roughly howled again. Kitty yowled.

Then a volley of ferocious barking and snarling broke out, as if all the dogs had escaped from their cages and were slaughtering each other. The cats screamed as if they were being skinned alive.

"Cut that out," Kelly said crossly, and jerked the leather thong.

Roughly twisted easily out of her grasp and howled again. The noise from the caged area became even louder and more alarming.

Kelly paled. "What's happening?" she gasped. "What's he doing to them? Make him stop or I'll call the police."

Jai scooped Kitty up off the desk. "Run," he said to Moon Unit.

Roughly bounded along next to them as they made a dash for the van. Moon Unit pulled open the doors. Jai climbed in with Kitty as Roughly leaped into the back. The doors slammed.

The engine stuttered and faded.

"Come on! Come on!" Moon Unit begged.

Jai looked behind him. Kelly appeared in the doorway,

shouting at them and waving her arms.

"Hurry, hurry," he shouted. The engine caught and began to turn over. With a loud backfire, the van took off.

Moon Unit was driving like a maniac. "Just hope she doesn't call the fuzz," he gasped to Jai.

"The fuzz?"

"The cops, the police."

"She seemed so nice," Jai said.

"She's got to follow rules, man, like everyone. That's what's wrong with the world, too many rules and too many people enforcing them." He shook his head. "That was a dreadful place. Like a concentration camp. All those beautiful creatures just waiting to be murdered. And how many of them are like your two. They're not really animals, are they? They're like you. Aliens from some other world."

Roughly growled.

"They aren't really aliens," Jai said. "They're animals, but they're a special sort of animal."

"They understand everything, don't they? Can they talk, too?"

"They can't talk here," Jai said, puzzled. "But in my world they take human shape and in their own world they can talk. That's why I have to get them back to Nexhoath and back to their own world."

"Far out," Moon Unit sighed. "This has to be the wildest day of my life. Other worlds, talking animals—I always knew all that stuff was real."

TWENTY-TWO

By the time they got back to Nexhoath the sky had clouded over, and a few drops of rain were beginning to fall. Apart from Moon Unit, who was still shaking his head and exclaiming "unreal" every few minutes, they were subdued and quiet. Kitty sat on Jai's knee, and he stroked her, but she didn't purr.

Jai's spirits sank even further when he saw the bay horse had disappeared from the paddock. Moon Unit didn't notice, but Roughly and Kitty exchanged a look of dismay. Roughly's ears and tail dropped, and Kitty dug her claws into Jai's knees without meaning to. She yowled mournfully.

Moon Unit parked the van in the barn, and they all climbed out. Jai wondered what he should do next. Where in the three worlds was Seal? And what shape was she now?

"Stay here," he told Kitty and Roughly, and they reluctantly sat down on the dusty floor.

"What do you want me to do?" Moon Unit asked. When Jai didn't reply immediately, he went on. "You're frightened of something, aren't you? What is it? Is someone after you?"

"It's the man you call Babaji," Jai said. "Can you go to the house and make sure he's not there?"

"Babaji? Do you know, I always thought there was something a bit phony about him. Okay." Moon Unit set off toward the back door. As he passed the paddock he stopped, as if surprised. He turned and called back to Jai. "That horse has disappeared again!"

Jai held his finger to his lips, hoping Moon Unit could see him and would shut up.

Moon Unit nodded vigorously and headed toward the house.

But before he got there the door flew open, and Seal tumbled out. She was wriggling and fighting against two bony, grasping hands.

"Babaji," Moon Unit said disapprovingly. "What are you doing to that child, man?"

Seal was distraught, at the end of her tether and exhausted. She was trying to change into something slippery, preferably a snake so she could bite Mr. Drake, but she simply did not have the strength.

"Let go of me! Let go of me!" she shrieked.

Kitty and Roughly heard her voice and came bounding out of the barn. They couldn't help themselves. They had to be near Seal.

Jai followed them.

Lightfoot rushed out of the kitchen like a small tornado.

"Leave that girl alone," she ordered Mr. Drake. She took hold of Seal and pulled her back into the kitchen. Jai, Kitty,

Roughly, and Moon Unit all trooped after them.

"Hi, Jai," Leaf called from the couch. He was still watching television.

Mr. Drake followed, exclaiming at the top of his voice, "She's a thief! She's stolen something from me!"

"I don't care what she did," Lightfoot snapped back at him. "You simply can't treat children like that."

"Where is it?" Mr. Drake shouted at Seal. "Where have you hidden it?"

The television was blaring loudly, and Lila was screaming her head off. Lightfoot turned off the television and picked the baby up. "This place is a madhouse. And where did all these animals come from?"

"They're mine," Seal replied, gathering Kitty into her arms. Roughly pressed close to her, tail wagging.

"You'd better go home, love," Lightfoot said to Seal. "And take your pets with you. Your parents will be worrying about you." She rocked the baby, trying to soothe her.

"No they won't," Seal said. "As a matter of fact, I haven't got any parents."

Moon Unit was studying her. "Where did you spring from?" he said. "Are you an alien, too?"

Lightfoot clicked her tongue and shook her head. "What are you on, mate? Do you think you could come down and get back to earth?"

"The boy's an alien," Moon Unit assured her. "And the animals can talk and everything."

"Dad," Leaf said, shrieking with laughter, "you really are losing the plot."

Moon Unit ignored him. "I think you were the horse," he said excitedly to Seal. "Oh, wow! You were the horse. Unreal!"

The baby, who had stopped crying for a few moments, started to grizzle again. She put her fists in her mouth and sucked on them.

"Her teeth hurt," Lightfoot said. "Get her the teething ring, Moon Unit."

Moon Unit reached into the cot and took out a bone ring. He handed it to Lila, who grasped it and put it in her mouth.

Lightfoot looked at it in surprise. "Not this one. The plastic one. Where did this come from?"

Mr. Drake and Seal both spoke together. "It's mine," they said, and put out their hands for it.

The baby looked at Mr. Drake. Her face puckered. Then she looked at Seal and smiled. Mr. Drake tried to snatch the ring. The baby yelled, frightened by the sudden movement. Lightfoot spun away from him and calmed Lila down. The baby grasped the ring tightly in her little fat hand. Then, still fretting a little, she held it out to Seal.

Seal took it gently. She placed her thumb on the smooth place next to the animal's face. "In Nexhoath the baby always holds the power," she said, speaking as if she did not know where the words were coming from.

Mr. Drake backed away, mouth tightening, eyes narrowed. He ran from the kitchen into the room next door, the housekeeper's sitting room. He wrenched his computer from the wall and snatched up his black clothes.

As he came out of the room again, Jai grabbed at his nightshirt. Mr. Drake wriggled out of it and ran in his underclothes toward the hall.

"Stop him, stop him," Jai shouted.

Leaf had followed Jai into the passage and he now tried to kick Mr. Drake as he scurried past.

"Let him go," Seal said. "He's going back to the ninth world. We can deal with him there."

"You're going back to another world? Can I come with you?" Moon Unit begged as they all, apart from Lightfoot, who stayed in the kitchen rocking Lila, flocked to the hall.

"No," Seal replied firmly. "Soon the gateway will be closed. Anyway, you have to stay and look after your baby here."

There was no sign of Mr. Drake, just the murals and the pyramid, and the chest with the closed lid. Seal opened it, and Roughly and Kitty jumped in.

"Come on, Jai," Seal said. "You can go home."

Jai hesitated. He was longing to go back to his own world, but there was so much he wanted to ask Leaf and Moon Unit about this one. The computers, the flying machines, the cars, the magic box, the lights that now lit the study brightly without any gas—they all seemed so fascinating and futuristic. He would love to understand how they worked.

"Come on," Seal said impatiently.

"Thanks for everything," Jai said to Moon Unit. "You saved all of us."

"It's cool," Moon Unit replied. "Anytime." He held out his hand. *"Hasta la vista,"* he said.

Leaf was staring, mouth agape. "I don't believe it," he said. "You mean Dad was right after all? You're aliens? I'll never hear the end of this. No wonder you didn't know anything! Hey, come back some time, Jai! We can swap info about our worlds!"

"I'd love to, but I don't think I'll be able to," Jai said as he stepped into the chest. He could hear Leaf and Moon Unit shouting good-bye. Seal followed him and closed the lid. Then she opened it, and they all climbed out into the hall again.

Jai felt a momentary pang of sadness as he imagined Leaf opening the chest in the tenth world and finding it empty.

The familiar smell of Nexhoath Nine hit them. The hall was deserted. The gas lamps hissed quietly. It was late afternoon and almost dark.

"Kitty and Roughly, you must go back to the eighth world," Seal said in a quiet, determined voice. "You need to rest and recharge."

"What about you?" Kitty said, relieved she could speak again. "You must be exhausted. You can't go on much longer."

"Come back and rest, too," Roughly added. "You can leave this world forever. Now that we have the ring, we can close the doorway."

"First I have to deal with Mr. Drake," Seal said, "and rescue Hugo."

Roughly looked at Kitty. She nodded almost imperceptibly. "Then we'll stay here with you," he said.

"Just go back to the eighth world quickly, so you can take human shape here," Seal said.

"We'd rather not leave you," Kitty yowled. "Not even for a little while."

The girl, the boy, the dog, and the cat headed for Mr. Drake's study. Through the hall windows an amber light began to glow. The Cat's Eye was rising.

Twenty-three

Mr. Drake was struggling into his black clothes. As the door opened he straightened his trousers and fastened the buttons at his neck. His hands fumbled a little. Jai noticed they were yellowish, and beginning to curve like claws. It made him look much older.

His voice was fainter and croakier, too, but his eyes brightened when he saw Jai.

"Just who I needed to see," he said, trying to assume the tones of the headmaster. "Jai Kala. We will resume where we left off."

"Don't go on like that," Seal interrupted. "We know who you are and what you do."

Mr. Drake ignored her, picking up the glass-eyed object that Jai now knew was called a camera, and aiming it at the boy.

The computer sat on the table, its screen alive and waiting.

Seal took the ring out of her pocket and moved to stand in front of Jai. "You are finished!" she shouted. "Go back to where you came from."

"You go back to where you came from," Mr. Drake

replied. "You and the animals, go back to your world. Just leave me Jai. He's the last one I need. Then the picture and my power here will be complete. He means nothing to you. He's not from your world. Why do you want to bother with him?"

"He's our friend," Seal said furiously. "And it's not only him. It's Hugo, and Fern, and Jamie, and Mr. Porteous, and all the others. I'm not going until they're released." She held up the ring, with her thumb against the half-animal face. "You know what gives this power? It's the animal and the human worlds working in harmony. That's what we have against you. Jai and I and Kitty and Roughly are all together. You can't defeat us now."

"You cannot defeat me, either. We are both strangers here," Mr. Drake whispered. "Here in the ninth world of Nexhoath, I think you'll find our powers are more or less equal. So go, and leave me with Jai." He broke off, swaying a little.

Roughly leaped at him. The dog knocked Mr. Drake off his feet. The camera flew from his hands. Jai caught it just before it hit the floor. Mr. Drake fell with a thump onto the carpet. Roughly jumped on his back, and Kitty sat on his head.

Mr. Drake hardly struggled. Jai realized the headmaster's power must be fading.

"Do you know how to use that thing, Jai?" Seal said.

"I think so. Leaf showed me."

Jai put the camera down on the desk. He had to choose a disk, which was what Leaf had called the cards, to insert into the computer. He picked one up at random. It was Mrs. Frumbose's.

"I hope nothing goes wrong," he muttered as he loaded it in. Mrs. Frumbose had never done anything to make him like her, but he still didn't want to destroy her completely.

Mrs. Frumbose's image came up on the screen, fractured into segments, just like Leaf's had been. Jai manipulated the pieces until she was whole again. Then he pressed the delete button.

Mr. Drake gave a whimper of pain. He began to writhe feebly, but Roughly and Kitty kept him pinned to the floor.

Jai ran to the door to look at the portrait. A dark space had appeared in its chest, over the heart. As he was gazing at it, Mrs. Frumbose came into the hall.

"Hello, dear," she said. "Are you getting on all right? Not too homesick?" Jai shook his head.

Mrs. Frumbose seemed to be on the verge of smiling. "I'm just going to make the children some chocolate cake for tea," she said. Then she did smile. Her face was transformed.

She disappeared in the direction of the kitchen, undoing the top button of her dress as she went.

"I think it worked," Jai cried, turning back into the study.

"Quick!" Seal exclaimed. "Do everyone else. Do Hugo!"

Jai went through the entire school, starting with Hugo and ending with Mr. Corio. As he restored and then deleted each of the images, a noise began to grow from the class-rooms. It was the noise of children released, children laughing and talking, joking and playing. It increased until it was almost deafening.

Then they heard Mr. Porteous calling above the hubbub, "Just a minute, girls and boys. A little bit quieter, please!" The din waned for a few moments.

As each future was restored, Mr. Drake became smaller, more contorted, older and weaker, until he lay on the carpet, eyes glittering with implacable hatred and rage, his true identity revealed—a monster, a twisted drackle from beyond the tenth world.

Jai went to check the portrait. The frame held only a black empty space.

"What are we going to do with him?" Seal said, gazing in revulsion at the former headmaster.

"Send him back to the tenth world," Roughly growled.

"No!" Jai protested, thinking of Moon Unit and Lightfoot, Leaf and Lila.

"Can we trap him in that thing?" Seal demanded, gesturing toward the computer.

Mr. Drake's body went into a spasm.

"I'll try," Jai said, lifting the camera and pointing it at him.

As he'd thought, the camera was linked to the computer. Mr. Drake's image appeared on the screen. Jai found an unlabeled disk and loaded it. He pressed some keys as Leaf had shown him. The computer made a little clicking noise as if it was thinking about something. Then Mr. Drake's image disappeared.

And so did Mr. Drake. One moment Kitty and Roughly were holding him down. The next, the carpet was empty. Jai went to the door. From the portrait the glittering eyes shone down, the drackle's image transferred into the empty picture.

"He hasn't really gone," Seal whispered. "What if he escapes from there?"

"Just have to make sure he never does," Jai said. He gave the picture one last look of revulsion and went back to the computer. He took the disk out and put it in his pocket. Then he turned the machine off.

"Drackles have no future of their own," he said slowly, remembering the old legends. "They have to steal other people's."

Seal hugged Roughly, and Jai hugged Kitty. Then they hugged each other.

"You did it, Jai," Seal shrieked. "You are so brilliant. You actually understood all that stuff."

"Good work," Roughly barked.

Kitty rubbed herself up against their legs, purring and purring.

A shout came from the hall. "Mr. Drake! I need to have a word with you!"

Kitty and Roughly hid quickly under the desk.

Mr. Porteous appeared on the threshold of the study. He looked around in surprise. "Where is that scoundrel?" He blinked hard as if he were seeing out of his own eyes for the first time in many months. "Where's Mr. Drake?"

Behind him the other teachers were gathering one by one. Miss Arkady was looking at her long slender hands in bewilderment. Mrs. Antrobus was patting at her hair, and Mr. Corio was pinching himself on the arm.

"Mr. Drake's gone," Jai said. "You used to be headmaster, didn't you, Mr. Porteous? I think you'd better take over again."

Mr. Porteous blinked at Jai like a bewildered owl. "Mr. Drake has been ruining the school," he said slowly. "I can't think why I didn't see it before. Why didn't I stop him?"

"He was very powerful," Seal said. "None of you was to blame."

Mr. Porteous spun around as a shriek of joy came from behind him. Jamie was flying down the banisters, followed by Hugo. On the top landing, two children were having a pillow fight. One of them was Fern, who had already changed into her black sweater and silver tights.

"Good Heavens," Mr. Porteous exclaimed. "Anarchy seems to have broken out. I'd better go and restore some order." He walked to the foot of the stairs, where Jamie and Hugo were lying in a heap, giggling.

"Boys," Mr. Porteous said firmly, "no sliding down the banisters. If you have so much energy, you can come and help me organize some indoor games before supper."

The boys jumped to their feet. Jamie went off cheerfully with Mr. Porteous. Hugo came toward Seal.

"Sardines!" suggested Mrs. Antrobus, hurrying after Mr. Porteous.

Miss Arkady ran after her and took her arm. "Or what about some dancing? I can play the piano."

Mr. Corio lingered in the doorway. "Celia," he said awkwardly. "I may have been a little harsh on you in the past. I hope we can make a new start."

"Well, you see . . . ," Seal began to explain.

A low growl came from under the desk.

"It's all right, Mr. Corio," she said, and smiled at him.

He smiled back. Music began to echo from the dining room. Mr. Corio glanced in its direction. "I might go and give them a hand," he said. "I don't suppose anyone except me knows how to dance the Lancers." As he turned to go, he looked back at Seal and added, "You know, I've often thought I've heard a dog at Nexhoath. But there aren't any dogs here, are there?"

Seal shook her head without saying anything.

"Come and join in, boys," Mr. Corio said. "Hugo? Jai?"

"In a minute," Hugo said.

Jai remembered the laptop computer lying on the desk, still open. He didn't think it was a very good idea to leave it there. He walked over to it and closed it, picked it up, and tucked it under his arm. He thought he would take the camera, too, just to prevent anyone else tinkering with it and accidentally releasing what was left of Mr. Drake.

When all the teachers and children had left the hall, Kitty and Roughly came out from under the desk. They sat and waited patiently while Hugo talked to Seal.

"I'm sorry I was so beastly to you," Hugo said, "and I'm sorry I gave your ring to Mr. Drake."

"You were never beastly," Seal said loyally, "and, anyway, beastly is a good word. It means like an animal!"

"Mr. Drake really was a drackle! And you and Jai destroyed him. I can't believe you actually did it. So Jai was someone special after all!"

Seal smiled. "He was. Very special. And Kitty and Roughly helped, too."

"Where are Kitty and Roughly? They disappeared. Mrs. Frumbose was furious!"

"They're here," Seal said, indicating the two animals in the shadows.

Hugo's jaw dropped. "They were really animals? No wonder we thought they were weird! But how on earth . . ."

"Jai can explain it all to you," Seal said. She sounded tired and a little sad. "But I have to say good-bye. I'm leaving with Kitty and Roughly."

Kitty nodded.

"Yes," Roughly said quietly. "It's time to go home."

Hugo looked more and more astonished. "I thought I heard that dog talk!"

"Jai will explain," Seal said again.

Hugo looked from one face to another. "And what's that about home? Seal doesn't have a home. She lives here, at Nexhoath."

"I do live at Nexhoath," Seal responded, "but not at Nexhoath Nine. Good-bye, Hugo. Thank you for being my friend when I had no other friends."

"Where are you going?" Hugo cried. "You can't go now, just when everything's worked out. Seal, you saved my life. You can't just leave me here now!"

"I have to go," Seal said. Her eyes were dark with unshed tears.

It was so strange, Jai thought, that Seal, who cried about everything, should not be crying now. He felt like crying, and Hugo looked as if he was about to burst into tears at any moment.

"Will I ever see you again?" Hugo demanded.

Seal looked at Kitty, then at Roughly. "Probably not," she said. "Unless things go wrong again."

"They won't," Roughly said with feeling.

"You can never tell," Seal said. "There's always the things the oddity makes you . . ." She stopped dead, and a look of amazement crossed her face. "Oh!" she said. "Oh, I've just realized something. Wait a moment!"

She ran to the front door and opened it.

"Where are you going?" Kitty yowled.

"There's someone else who needs to go home," Seal

shouted as she disappeared into the darkness.

They all ran to the door and stared out after her. Beneath the light of the radiant Cat's Eye, the grounds of Nexhoath lay silent and beautiful.

A few minutes later they heard the sound of horses' hooves.

Seal reappeared, leading Midnight and Starlight. The two horses came nervously into the hall, dropping their heads and looking very ashamed when they saw Kitty and Roughly.

"It's all right," Seal said soothingly. "Everything's forgiven now. You can go home."

Kitty said, "They're your guardians!"

"The poor things were trapped here," Seal said. "They couldn't get back to the chest, and they'd been here so long, they couldn't talk, either."

She opened the lid of the chest and first Midnight, then Starlight, put their front hooves in, shrank, and slid into the chest. Seal closed the lid on them.

"We'll deal with them when we get back," Roughly growled.

"No, you mustn't," Seal said. "I'm sure they've been punished enough. They must have recognized me when I came back, but they could never tell me. I don't suppose they've been very well treated here. I've forgiven them, and you must, too."

"Well, all right," Roughly agreed.

Seal patted him. "Good boy! Now it really is good-bye!" She hugged first Hugo and then Jai.

"Thank you," Kitty said to Jai. "We thought you were the one, and you weren't, but we never could have done it without you."

Roughly licked Jai's hand wordlessly.

Seal lifted the lid of the chest. Kitty and Roughly jumped in.

"Look out for the Dead Baby!" Hugo tried to laugh, to stop the tears.

"The Dead Baby's at rest now," Seal said. "Everything's back as it should be. Good-bye," she said again. She stepped into the chest and pulled the lid shut.

"Don't go!" Hugo ran to open it. Beneath his fingers, the crack in the lid closed over. He jumped back, white and shaking. "Seal! Seal!"

"Don't be sad," Jai said. "She's gone home."

Hugo went back to the chest, felt the now solid wood of the lid, opened it, reached inside. It was empty. He crouched down, peered underneath it, looked behind it.

"They've gone to another world," Jai said. "It's where Seal belongs. She'll be happy there. I'll explain it all to you.

"And look," he said to Hugo, showing him the computer. "This is what Mr. Drake was using. I'm going to try to find out how you make them. And there's something around called electricity. I'm going to discover that, too."

He looked around the hall. From the other part of the

house they could hear shouts of laughter. A sudden draft made the candles in the chandelier flicker. Their light fell on the portrait. Mr. Drake's eyes looked down on Jai, as evil and glittering as they had been when they had shone from the drackle's body on the carpet in the study.

Jai shivered and clasped the computer closer to him. He would never, ever let Mr. Drake escape. For a moment he felt terribly alone. No one else would ever understand about the other worlds, stretching away from Nexhoath. No one else would ever know the adventure he had shared with Seal, Kitty, and Roughly.

Kitty had been right. He had been through the gateway between the worlds, and it had changed him forever.

Hugo was staring at him, almost as if he was aware of it. He looked as if he was going to say something to Jai, but before he could speak, they heard noises outside—footsteps, and voices, and then the door knocker: *bang! bang! bang!*

The letter slit opened and closed. There was a little *tap tap tap* on the step, as if someone were dancing on it. Jai ran to open the door.

Sunita stood there, her dark eyes sparkling. "Jai," she gasped. "How wonderful, you aren't in school uniform yet! We must have gotten here in time."

Behind Sunita stood a smiling man who looked so like her, he had to be her father. The huge black car stood in the driveway, its lanterns burning dully. In their light Jai could see Canvey holding open the back door so the passengers could step out. First his mother, then his father.

"This is Daddy," Sunita said. "I told you he could fix everything. He got your parents off the ship. Everything's settled. They're going to get their visas so they can stay here, and we've come to take you home."

Jai's first instinct was to run and throw himself into his mother's arms, but he was still holding the computer and the camera. He wasn't sure he would ever be able to let go of them.

With that knowledge heavy in his heart, he walked down the steps to greet his parents.